# WORLD WAR II

## BOOK TWO

# DEAD IN THE WATER

## CHRIS LYNCH

SCHOLASTIC PRESS ★ NEW YORK

ISBN 978-0-545-67598-7
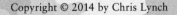
10 9 8 7 6 5 4 3 2 1          14 15 16 17 18
Printed in the U.S.A.                    23
First edition, October 2014

The text type was set in Sabon.
Book design by Christopher Stengel

<br>

## CHAPTER ONE
# One Torpedo

Every man should be prepared to lose one son in a fight to defend his own."

That is my Pop talking to me. To me and my brother, Theo. But that almost goes without saying. Naturally he is speaking to me *and* Theo, because the last time anybody said anything to me without Theo being close enough to hear every word was when I was one year old. Then he was born.

We're kinda close.

Anyway, that is Pop talking to my brother and myself as we stand in the front hall with the door wide open, the two of us just heading off to sign up to fight in the war that everybody knows is coming.

It is a shocking thing to hear, to say the least, on the way to do what we are on the way to do. It sounds like he is giving us up, throwing us to the sharks in the name of patriotism.

But of course he's doing no such thing. This, in fact, is Pop being as soft and emotional as I have ever seen him. He has more to say. The reason we have to keep standing there in the open doorway and wait for him to say the rest of it is because he is choking on that first part. So he starts again, but faster this time.

"Every man should be prepared to lose one son in a fight to defend his own. But no one should have to lose two."

Now it makes sense. Though, perhaps not to my mam. None of it makes sense to her. Which is why she is elsewhere today, bawlin' her eyes out to her own mam.

It is usually Theo's job to lighten stuff up when stuff gets all grim. And he is frequently kept busy with that task since my father, as fine and upright a man as there ever was, can also be the very definition of what is known as *The Dour Scotsman*.

"Ah, nobody's dyin', Pop," Theo says, laughing, waving our old man off and sauntering out the door. As if he thinks that will end it.

"Everybody's dying, Theodore," Pop intones — because that's what he does; he intones. He intones in such a tone, without even raising his volume, that the pavement shakes under my brother's feet and freezes him there as surely as if he'd been seized by the ankles.

"Sorry, Pop," Theo says, turning slowly back toward us.

"Don't be sorry, and don't be stupid. People are getting killed everywhere and every way in this bloody mess, and the surest way to join them is to go thinking that you somehow know something that the Brits and the Poles and the French and all those other sorry souls don't know. Do you know such a thing, my son, that you would like to share with the rest of the world before it's too late, if in fact it's not too late already?"

I believe there have been entire months during which my father has not spoken that many words.

"No, sir," Theo says, wisely. "I know no such thing."

Pop exhales then, releasing the lungfuls of air he had stored up in case more speech was required.

"Good," Pop says, softly. Then, he gets to his point-of-points. "Henry," he says to me, never much liking the nickname *Hank* outside of birthdays and holidays and such. "You're set on the Navy, correct?"

"I am, Pop."

He nods. "It's a fine and noble service." Pop himself sailed, fine and nobly, in the Great War.

"Me too, Pop," Theo calls out. "It's the Navy for me, too." It is a frantic attempt to head off what he knows must be coming.

"No, Son," Pop answers.

"Pop!" Theo shouts.

This would not be something my brother — or

anyone else I know — would normally try on our father. I brace for the wrath.

But it doesn't come.

Pop shakes his head very slowly instead. He opens his mouth to explain, then looks down at his feet. He continues to look down as he speaks, haltingly.

"One torpedo . . ." he says. "One. Just the one, and that's . . ." His head starts shaking again. Then his hands, until he balls them into death-white fists and knocks them against his thighs. "We could never bear that. Thinking about that . . . every day, every night . . . I've seen torpedoes, up close, and their work, up close. . . ."

"But the buddy system," Theo pleads. "We'll be able to look out for each other."

"He's not your buddy, Theodore. He's your blood."

Desperate, Theo tacks the other way entirely. "They'll never put us on the same ship anyway, Pop."

"Yeah," I say, but with a lot less emphasis, a lot less expectation.

Then, a little curveball. Pop starts laughing. He looks up, shows us his rare red-rimmed eyes, shows his deep-creased face and mouth stretched in pride and stubborn admiration. "If there was any way, you two would make it happen. If you made it as far as the recruiting office together, you would make it happen somehow, of that I have no doubt."

It is, in the combination of the words and the manner, the warmth and the threat, titanic praise from the titan himself.

And it is also, definitively, the last word on the matter. My brother and I will not be enlisting in the same service. The logic of the argument is almost certainly my mother's, the steely resolve my father's, the combination an irresistible force.

He puts a big gentle hand on my back, eases me out to where Theo stands mute, and shuts the door firmly behind me.

## CHAPTER TWO

# Catch Across the World

**H**ow did he know?" Theo rants as we head down the road toward the bus station that will take us to our respective recruiting offices in Baltimore. "We were so good. We never let on, ever, what we were thinking. *Months*, we kept it under wraps, then — just as we're about to pull it off — *bam*! It's like he decoded us or something."

I have to laugh, grabbing him by the back of the head and shoving him farther up the sidewalk. "You have to admit, Theo, it wouldn't have taken the fanciest figurin' to work me and you out. Half of Accokeek probably decoded us before we even decoded ourselves."

Accokeek, Maryland. Home. It's small and it's tight and one time in high school I clobbered a lazy fastball so hard it broke a window in George Washington's house across the river in Mount Vernon. Before the ball even came to a stop every last person in Accokeek knew about it. Everybody knows everything here. Everybody knows us.

It is a long and solemn bus trip, a whole different journey than the one we thought we were taking when we were both Navy-bound. Then, before Pop split us up, we were just heading up the road, arm in arm to the same place with the same outcome. Now, Baltimore could just as well have been Bombay with how far it feels, and how foreign.

We both have to get used to it. But especially Theo, who has little more than an hour to decide which of the three remaining services will be his.

The bus cranks down to a stop in the big town, and we slowly make our way off along with about ten other folks who seem to share our general grimness about the whole thing.

But that's it. Time is up on me and Theo feeling sorry about this situation.

"Go on," I say firmly to my brother as he follows me toward my destination. *Destination* is perhaps too strong a word, as I am following my nose and nothing else down toward the water. But the one thing we do know for sure is that our destinations are not going to be the same. We have to adjust to that starting right now, and as the older brother this is my duty.

"Go on, what?" he says, wide-eyed as I set my hand flat on his chest. "Go on, what? Where?"

"Don't know," I say. "But I'll see you at home. Later."

I give him the littlest bitty shove backward as I nod toward the heart of old Baltimore. But I might as well have heaved him off the side of a cliff, judging by the lost and hurt look he gives me before I force myself to turn away and not see it. I know he is still standing there as I march away from him. I know he is staring at the back of me and is bewildered.

But my brother is tough, with or without me. I know that. We both have to know it.

He is sitting on the front steps as I come walking up the path toward the house a few hours later. He has his baseball glove on and is smacking a ball into it over and over again, so hard you could close your eyes and think it was the A's batting practice going on back in Federalsburg.

"Well, 'bout time," he says. "I was starting to wonder if we were gonna have enough daylight left for a little throwin'. You Navy boys sure do take your time cruising back and forth to a situation."

It's closing in on sundown. But all things considered, I thought I'd made pretty good time from Baltimore, up and back and what all in between.

I shrug. "Sailors," I say, reaching up just in time to

catch my own glove that he's slung at me. "We do have our own pace."

Theo nods, knowingly. There is either a brand-new wisdom about his whole manner since I left him on that Baltimore street, or a brand-new ability to approximate it. I don't suppose there's a significant difference, as far as I am concerned.

We start playing catch, quiet at first. Slow and easy. This will not last long, that much is for sure, so we enjoy it while we can.

This is it for us, our thing. Catch. I don't think we have gone two days without playing, not since we got our first mitts. That was on a Christmas morning, back when we were so small it was an achievement simply to keep the gloves upright and hope the ball just dropped in there. It was snowing steady that day, and we were slipping and stumbling all over the place, but we didn't care. Just like all those days since then, when we didn't care if it was snowing or raining or roasting or hurricaning, and we would play catch. And talk. And catch, and figure, and catch, and sort. Catch.

"So," I say, after enough time and forty-some throws have passed between us without him telling me about his enlistment. "What did you think, by the way, of Pop's theory? About being prepared to lose one son?"

*Snap.*

That's the stuff now. He is putting some mustard on his throws now, so this is the real talk coming.

"Didn't think much about it at all, really," he says. "I just assumed he meant you."

"Ha!" I say, pointing at him with my glove hand before letting fly with a sizzler right at his face.

He catches it easy and with a big grin on his mug. He did grow up a lot since I left him there in the big city, working it out on his own.

"So?" I say, finally, giving in to him and asking for the answer. "Where you goin', boy?"

Still smiling, and with the ball gripped for the throw, he releases one finger and points at the sky.

Army Air Corps.

For some deep, unknown reason, this makes me very satisfied, thinking of Theo soaring up there above it all. His own helpless grinning is probably a big part of my satisfaction. I open my mouth for a follow-up interrogation, but he is already done with that. He whips the ball back at me, shutting my mouth and taking the conversation where he prefers it.

"You're not gonna tell the whole world that president's-window nonsense when you're over there, are ya?" Theo says as the ball pops hard into my glove.

"Of course I am," I say, sending one whistling back his way. The ball makes a crack-snap as he gloves it right beside his ear without hardly twitching. "You saw it with your own eyes, too. It was incredible, and *should* be talked about."

He sends the ball back in a blink, like he's turning a double play. Then he lets his arms drop straight down by his sides, which is always his way of showing a lack of respect for the proceedings. "That pop-up wouldn't have reached the shortest fence in the whole Eastern Shore League. *And* it was a foul ball."

I whip the ball back at him, forcing those dubious hands right back up to protect that dubious face. "Washington's window. Get it right, tell it right. And I'm expecting you to spread my legend over there, too, wherever *over there* turns out to be for you."

We are interrupted then by a piercing voice from the second-floor window.

"Over there? Over there, over where, over there?" It is like heckling from the grandstands, only much harder to ignore.

That is our little sister, Susan, and her voice has every right to be piercing. It is gonna get a whole lot worse, too, because she is ten years old and idolizes both of us and we have been doing a bad thing to her out of fear.

We have been keeping the enlistment plan from her. Theo and I both agreed that we are a lot more scared of Susan than of whatever we are gonna run into overseas.

"Snoozie Suzie, how long you been listening to us?" Theo calls up, all play on the outside but surely all pudding on the inside.

"Too long, that's how long. I shoulda stopped when I was about five. But since I didn't have the sense then, why don't I just keep listenin' now while you tell me where the *over there* is that you're takin' that stupid George-Washington-broken-window-fat-lie story to."

Because we are good under pressure, my brother and me, we start throwing the ball back and forth crazy fast like we are in a game of pepper or something, but neither one of us has words to give to a ten-year-old girl who certainly deserves some. Maybe because her strong and sharp words sank into a sad, cracky warble, which is definitely not our sister's way. Maybe because we know that she knows what we are hiding, and we all know how it is gonna go from here.

"Right," Susan says to the big, strapping ballplayers who are switching uniforms to go put the world and the war to rights. "I'm comin' down there."

It shames me a little bit to admit that I am truly considering running. But only a little. Susan is a fearsome force, I tell you what. But if I am gonna learn honorable behavior and facing up to fear, this is the very place to start.

Theo has his arms open wide as she comes running out of the house full throttle toward him. This is their game, and it is always fifty-fifty whether or not she is going to knock him backward, even though he does not ever purposely give in. I can feel the earth rumble beneath my feet as she thunders past me, gaining speed and heading for the inevitable.

Theo, glove on, eyes closed, is smiling and wincing both as she reaches him.

And she stops cold.

He holds his eyes shut. She reaches up and peels them open.

"You got something to tell me, Theodore?" Susan says, deep and deadly.

He closes his eyes again. She runs quickly out of humor, folds her arms, and waits.

By the time my brother gathers up the courage to open his eyes, there are tears coming from them. The two of them are weeping. All right, all right, there are three of us at it then.

Pop has always been one of the most practical men on earth. One of the things he did to make Theo and me among the best defensive infielders in the game was spend hours and hours drilling us. What he drilled us with was tennis balls. He'd line us up along the back wall of the house and from about twenty feet away he would serve us bombs like he was Don Budge or something. Where he got the balls, the racket, or the ability to serve like that was anybody's guess since he barely recognized tennis as a sport. Except, that is, when Budge would win a major tournament someplace and Pop would remind us that Budge's father was a Scot.

He hit those balls at us relentlessly, 'til we had welts all over our bodies — and our faces. We had to field them glovelessly, and wordlessly, until his trash barrel of balls was empty, and then we had to collect them all up and feed them back to the beast so the beast could welt us some more. We had to field them and field them until we could catch every catchable ball and then until we could redefine what was catchable and catch all of the rest as well. Nobody had hands like us. Because nobody had a pop like Pop.

He is that serious and practical about most things, and that includes religion. We have always been a pious and churchgoing family. Despite that, I couldn't tell you what exactly my father believes or doesn't believe, because on that subject he remains as silent as snow.

Because on all matters Episcopal, there is one head of the McCallum congregation, and that is Mam.

I'm not sure myself whether I believe in God in any of the forms I have been made aware of. But I believe in Mam, and by that same power I have no trouble thinking of myself now and forever as Episcopalian. Whatever I go on to see in this world, it's never going to be convincing enough to get me to unsee what my mother has shown me.

"Listen hard, my boys," Mam says as we all walk together to our last Sunday service before Theo and I ship out. "Whatever the Reverend has to say today should sustain you through your trials, on your travels, until we are all able to listen to him together once more."

"Yes, ma'am," I say.

"Should we not heed what the chaplains have to say in the meantime?" Theo teases.

Pop clips him in the back of the head. Sounds just like snapping fingers. Not his, of course, since my father has never in his life used his fingers for anything as frivolous as snapping.

"Heed," Mam says. "Do heed. Especially you, Theodore. But home, family, your church, your parish — that's what you're to remember deepest and hold dearest. That's what'll keep you. It's what'll keep *us*."

And that is that for that. Sunday is for *listening* — it is one of Mam's tried and trues. We walk in peace the rest of the way, and we sit listening hard once we get there.

Listening hard, but listening to what? Distant guns and foreign tongues. "Anchors Aweigh," the Navy's fight song, which I could swear I am hearing clearly from the academy just up the way. Annapolis is right around the corner according to the map but still too far away to be hearing a bunch of cadets singing. Yet I can hear it, clear and loud and immediate. How could anybody hear anything from the pulpit in that situation?

". . . and farewell to two more of Maryland's finest, Henry and Theodore McCallum, joining the effort to do Our Lord's work in this terrible fight . . ."

That would be one way. As attention grabbers go, I can't think of a time when Reverend Jenkins topped this.

There is a bubbling of low murmur throughout the church, which in this place is the equivalent of a standing ovation in a baseball park. Susan, I see out of the corner of my eye, is turning every which way to make out what all the fuss is about until Mam grabs her arm and stills her. Our folks are looking down at the floor, refusing to acknowledge anything because for them that would be immodest. But I slide a glance to my right at Theo, and he slides one left at me, and we both nod, an appreciation to the congregation even if we aren't strictly looking at any of them. They get it, though, because that is pretty well how communications get exchanged in Prince George's County.

We certainly pay attention now, since this is the first time we have ever been the actual subject of a sermon, and the only time we are ever likely to be.

". . . a dauntingly hard road ahead for our brave boys," Reverend Jenkins intones. "Against long and frightening odds, and a lamentably sad task it will be, regardless . . ."

I am beginning to get really worried for us, now that the Reverend is stating our case. Fortunately, Theo is on hand for perspective.

He leans in close to my ear. "That's nothing. Doesn't he realize we played in the farm system of the Philadelphia A's? Every single game is dauntingly hard for the A's."

"Ha!" escapes my mouth just before I manage to clap a hand over it. The entire congregation bears down on me with stares, starting with my mother, swinging around the whole church, and ending with my mother. Never mind the Pacific Theater of Operations, I might not make it out of Christ Episcopal Church in one piece.

Fortunately, just as the Reverend Jenkins giveth our problem, the Reverend taketh it away.

"Ha, indeed," he says, gesturing with open arms toward my brother and me. "Have we ever seen such bravery?"

And this time we get applause, the real kind, and the contours of the church and the strangeness of this response make the whole thing sound like the structure is going to crumble and crash down around us.

It is a sensation I am probably going to have to get used to. And learn to disregard.

"But!" Reverend Jenkins admonishes, waving a finger at the whole population as they settle back down, then waving it specifically at the brothers McCallum. "Your bravery will get you far. But not so far that you can ever leave your humanity, and your Christianity, behind. As the Lord said in the Gospel of Matthew, chapter five, verse forty-four, *I say unto you, love your enemies, bless them that curse you, do good to them that hate you, and pray for them which despitefully use you, and persecute you.*"

The congregation has gone more silent now than at any time since we arrived. Quieter, I imagine, than it was before anyone arrived.

"It is what separates us from them. It is what will show our enemies the righteous way, the life, and the light, that guides us, and will someday guide them all out of their darkness. Do God's work, men. Do the sorrowful and the necessary, but never forget your Christian selves while you do it."

I have never heard the Reverend like this. I don't know if he has ever sounded like this, whether maybe he sounded like this every week and I just hummed my way through it until he directed it to me specifically. But he has my attention now, my brother's and sister's and probably Hitler's and Emperor Hirohito's, too, as he winds down the service and sends us out into the wide world.

The procession out of the church is likewise nothing like I have ever experienced here before. It's like the most solemn and peculiar wedding of all time, as Theo and I are the last to exit, with all the other families of the congregation there outside on the steps like a receiving line. All waiting to shake our hands and pat our backs and well-wish us down onto the sidewalk, across the street, and back on the road from Christ Episcopal to the old home one more time.

The quiet among the family feels different this time. We walk, as usual, in contemplative quiet. The contemplation, though, is not the usual.

Susan seems softly agitated, straining to keep to our studied, slow Sunday pace while she slaps her open palms nervously against her thighs. Mam is solemn as ever, but with a bit of something different, an almost prideful tilting back of her head. We will never know, though, never hear what she is thinking or feeling because that is just not her way.

Pop's way, of course, is always going to be Sunday silence. No reason to expect anything different today, even as different as today is. So we aren't looking for anything. Sure aren't looking for *this*:

"Any man who loves his enemies is not functioning properly," he says toward the ground, like he is telling it to Satan himself down there. He says it in a voice that makes Reverend Jenkins sound like a first-grade girl. "And any man at *war* who loves his enemies is insufficiently interested in coming home again."

Coming home again. That is the steely and stoic man's concern. And his message.

Now, nobody stops walking or breathing, though those are exactly the things that make the most sense at the time. We keep leaning homeward, but I surely feel the eyes of Susan and Theo on me, wondering: *What on earth do we do here?* Sidelong, I note the positions of both my parents, just ahead of the children per usual and per correctness. This is a declaration of war itself here, and something is almost certain to erupt as Mam turns slightly but definitely toward the side of her husband's head. Her cheeks are rose-red, her tight lips violet blue.

For his part, the old man keeps walking, head down, no more words coming from him, but an unmistakable low, low growl coming up. A growl.

Not toward Mam; never, never. But a growl all the same, a statement of seriousness I would bet he is unaware he is even making.

We wait.

We walk, and we wait.

And we walk on. Mam stops looking at him, and he stops growling. He has never once spoken up about God or the Reverend or the Church or the message before.

But we never had before what we have now.

She reaches sideways without looking at him, and takes his hand.

Another Sunday something that never happened before.

I don't know whether I sleep at all. My waking dreams and my sleeping dreams have all joined up together into one long barrage of heavy cannon fire, fighter planes swooping overhead, machine guns, and yelling. What I do know is that my gear is packed and it is just after daybreak when I head downstairs. I carry my glove and the battered ball, the brutally scarred baseball that I would throw against the jagged stone foundation of the house on the rare occasions when my brother was not available to throw with. It was a tremendous exercise for the reflexes, in that the wall's irregularities meant the ball never came back true. But it was a second-rate exercise, too, because with Theo the ball always came back true.

I won't have to go through it this morning, however, because by the time I get to the wall, the kid himself, my double play partner, is already there waiting. We won't be playing one more game of catch, though, either. His glove is on the ground, and he's not alone.

"Line up, boys," Pop says with almost a smile on his thin lips. He's standing by his trusty rusty barrel, a tennis ball in one hand and a racket in the other. "Can't be letting your skills erode just because of some war. Baseball will be waiting for you when you return."

"Sure, Pop," Theo says, which our father takes as some kind of starter's gun.

And gun he does. It is almost like he's mad at us for something, the way he booms shot after shot at us, taking no time at all between serves. He grunts like a wild boar as he throws himself into each shot, harder than the last.

And we are up to the task, let me say. Like giant spiders, like light-footed, sticky-fingered, spring-loaded alien athletes from Mars, we snag *every single* ball the old man launches. At my face, snagged. At Theo's feet, snagged. Ranging far, left and right, snagged and snagged, until Pop starts breathing real heavily and we start doing the grunting for him, growling and yapping as we amaze even ourselves with what is possible.

Until, at one point I become aware of Theo's soft hands hardening. He drops a ball. Then another. He is dropping balls, missing them entirely, having them pound off his chest, his arms. His primal grunting transforms, too, into something weaker, something wounded.

"Catch the balls, Theo," I say calmly, as if I wasn't saying the most obvious and unhelpful thing I could think of.

"I'm trying," he says, almost whispery.

"Catch the balls," I say, same as before. "Catch the balls. Catch them. Like we do. Catch them." All the while I keep catching them. Feel like I could close my eyes and not miss a one.

But if I'd done that I would have missed Theo's return, his bounce, his lunge, his snag. He has it again, he is right again. We are right.

Until it is done. The barrel is empty, our father wheezing, hands on his knees and a grimace of pure love and pride on his face. We stand upright, a small sea of fuzzy white balls rolling in the yard around our feet.

"It's just about that time, Pop," I say when he eventually straightens up.

He nods, with his hands on his hips now as they should always be. "Not before you pick up these balls. You're not going anywhere just yet. The war can just wait another minute while you do as you're told right here."

"Yes, sir," we say in unison, as we have done hundreds of thousands of times, and as we will now be saying separately, to other commands from other men, hundreds of thousands more times. We'll never mean it as much as we do now, though.

"And make it quick, because your mother wants to line me up for a few shots when you leave. She serves harder than I do, too. Ah, but fair enough, so. I can at least absorb this for her, eh?"

"Eh, Pop," Theo says, stuffing balls back into the barrel.

"Eh, Pop," I say, doing the same.

When the balls are all collected, Pop nods at the barrel, like he approves, like he needed to see the task through and now it is. I look up to see Mam at the window, washing away at some mystery dishes in her spotless pre-breakfast kitchen.

When she notices the three of us standing there like pointless oafs, she dries off her hands, then disappears from view. A couple of minutes later she reappears, coming around from the front of the house, rather than through the door right by the kitchen. Susan is with her, and each one of them is carrying one of our bags.

"Gee, rush us out, why don'tcha?" Theo says, laughing.

Mam drops the bag, walks right up to him, and slaps his face. It is not one of her meaningful slaps, but still it is an attention getter.

"No swearing. I don't care if you are in the Army now. You'll leave here with the manners you were taught, and you will return with them, too."

"Army Air Corps," he says, grinning.

*Slap.*

"Yes, ma'am." He coughs, squashed in her spontaneous strangle-hug.

She kisses his cheek hard, turns away from him quick. It is like one fluid motion, like she is turning a double play, as she swings into me, squeezes me 'til I think my eyeballs will pop right out, and then heads wordlessly, but quietly sobbing, back to her kitchen the direct way.

Pop shakes my hand, and bites his lip. He shakes Theo's hand, still biting. Then he heads for the kitchen door as well. Mam watches him, already back in position dishwashing. There'll be no enamel left on anything by the time we return.

"You know that thing," Susan says, picking up one bag and jamming it into Theo's hand. Then she shoves him in the back, in the direction of the war.

"What thing?" I say, similarly given my marching orders.

"That thing, about loving your enemy. About never forgetting you are a Christian and never forgetting who you are. That thing."

"Oh, that thing," Theo says as we round the corner of the house, out toward the road.

"That thing, yeah," she says. "Well, you forget it. That's the thing *I* want you to do, and you have to do it, do this one thing for me because you owe me. You owe me because of what you're doing to me. So that's the one thing I'm asking . . . I'm *telling* you to do for me. Just forget all that. Right?"

"Forget all what?" I say.

"There," Theo says. "Forgotten already."

"How many times do you need to get slapped?" she says, vicious serious.

"Sorry, Sue," he says.

"Don't bother being sorry. And don't bother being Christian. You hear me? You go ahead and forget who you are, and go on and kill. Kill everybody you need to.

Kill 'em all, understand? Kill everybody, and then come home. You can be Christian later. When Mam's watching."

Theo, because of nerves or stupidity or confusion, starts laughing. Which makes Susan start tearing up, which always makes her roar with rage. She hates to show that stuff. The Armed Services of the United States of America has no idea that they aren't getting the toughest McCallum we have, not by a long shot.

He really is itching for a slapping, so I do my bit. I slap my brother in the back of the head.

"I promise, Susan," I say, and lean in to hug her.

She shoves me away, hard, points menacingly at Theo.

"Promise me," she demands.

"I promise," he says. "Everything that moves."

"Good," she says, stomping her way back to the house already.

"I *hate* you," she shouts before slamming the door.

"Don't forget to write," Theo calls back.

We know she's heard him when the door swings open again, and we hotfoot it out onto the road with Susan's roar rattling our ear bones.

"Did you mean to bring that?" I say to him when we are out of range, out of sight of home. I point at his mitt, curled around a baseball and tucked under his arm.

"Of course I meant to bring it," he says. "How does a guy pick up a ball and glove *accidentally*? I was thinking about what that meathead said."

"Well, we've heard a lot of meatheads say a lot of things, so could you be more specific?"

"The meathead. Played first base, Centreville Red Sox."

"Right, with the gimpy ankle. Bucyk. Girlfriend tried to strangle me."

Theo smiles. "Hmm. Kinda liked her, though."

"Yeah, me too," I say.

"Right, anyway. Roman Bucyk, that's the guy. Meathead, of course; Sox. But what he said about the Nazis . . ."

"Nazis hate baseball."

"Nazis hate baseball! Exactly. So I figure, let's bring the game with us, save the world and drive them demented by playin' ball all the way."

I find myself nodding and shaking my head at the same time. "You know the enemy is wicked when they get us taking Red Sox advice."

"Ha," he says, "well, if we do this thing right the Sox will be waiting when we return. One evil empire at a time."

"Okay, brother," I say, feeling my own ball and glove under my arm. "It's just, I was thinking I would take the gloves with me."

"You? Why you? Can you even play catch on a boat?"

"Better than you can on a plane, flyboy."

"We're on solid ground most of the time. Which is more than you can say. I should probably take them. I'll play catch for both of us."

Suddenly, as we walk, and the bus crests the hill in the distance, this all becomes realer than ever, and unsettling in a way I didn't anticipate.

Not two days. We haven't gone two days without throwing a baseball back and forth to each other, and at each other.

I hand him my glove. Feels like I just tore my own arm off.

As the bus pulls up all crank and squeal and dust, Theo starts shaking his head.

"We can't do this," he says. I see the bus door open behind him.

"Well, we did enlist," I say. "I think they'll be mad if we say we were only joking."

"Not that," he says. "This." His bag is on the ground between his feet, and he is holding each glove up in one hand. "We have to play catch, Hank."

"Catch?" I say. "Across the world? Well, I could probably reach, but do you think your arm's up to it?"

"Ha," he says, shoving a glove back at me. "That's it, exactly. Catch across the world. Wherever we are, we'll play catch across the world."

"Any day now, gentlemen," the bus driver barks.

I take the glove, and put my hand on my brother's back, guiding him up the steps.

"But this is your glove," I say, noticing the relacing Theo does obsessively every year.

"I know," he says. "That's so you don't forget me."

"Ha," I say, and shove him a little harder.

We've been sitting, side-by-side and silent, with our mitts in our laps for fifteen minutes. It's like we're on one more road trip to another unfriendly ballpark, getting our game faces on, thinking about the competition. Then Theo reaches over and plunks the other glove into my lap.

"What are you doing?" I ask.

"I'll find something else to use for the duration," he says while staring straight ahead. "This set should stay together. Keep 'em together, Hank."

He is still not looking at me, at a point when I need to be responding somehow. But I just nod anyway, and I know that is enough.

PART TWO
THE SEA

## CHAPTER THREE
# Aweigh

The Chesapeake Bay was a bathtub compared to this. I thought it was big, I truly did. Before I saw that, I thought the Potomac River was big.

Now there is this. Now we are leaving one ocean for another, larger ocean.

We're passing through the Panama Canal, aboard the aircraft carrier USS *Yorktown*. The Canal is like a gigantic straw, sucking us from the Atlantic Ocean into the Pacific, where recent events have made it imperative that our naval firepower be. Those events would be the mauling of our Pacific fleet at Pearl Harbor in a surprise attack by the Japanese Imperial Navy. Sounds like a very dignified title for a bunch that behaves like that, if you ask me.

We were stationed at Norfolk, Virginia, when the attack happened, preparing for repairs after the battering we'd taken from North Atlantic storms. I was close enough to home that I could practically have shouted from the flight deck and kept in contact with my family.

When we got the call to action, I watched the Chesapeake Bay recede from me. As we steamed south, the bay that had seemed so big to me shrank to nothing, the Potomac beyond it getting silly small as the wide ocean gathered us up. The Atlantic's size embarrassed the waters of my youth, and it occurred to me that the *Yorktown* was already the biggest town I had ever lived in. The population of the ship smothers that of Accokeek.

We have more cobblers and bakers, too.

But anyway, flowing from the Atlantic into the Pacific gives me, finally, more than any moment so far, an appreciation of the *scale* of what is happening. Happening to me, happening to the world. To be even more strictly factual, we are flowing from the Caribbean, which is in a way a great big lagoon of the Atlantic, into the Gulf of Panama, which is the Pacific version of the same thing. Bodies of water that are vast to my experience, but little pools of not-much in the big-big scheme of things.

We had been *sort of* participating in the war prior to December 7, but there was an undefined awkwardness to our function as we all waited for whatever was to come. We were chugging up and down our sector of the Western Atlantic as part of a convoy protecting British merchant ships. These were called *Neutrality Patrols*, which was a funny and fuzzy way of looking at it. We were there protecting one side against the other — which doesn't sound very neutral at all, but what do I know. The Germans were similarly confused by the situation and expressed this by having one of their sneaky U-boats sink one of our destroyers, the *Reuben James*, which may or may not have been just minding its own business in the company of British shipping interests near Iceland.

And then, just over a month later, something got the Japanese all kinds of mixed up, because they bombed half the heart of our naval forces at Pearl Harbor in Hawaii.

From what I understand they had actually hoped to do a good bit better than that. They were disappointed not to find any of our carriers on the scene that day. Terribly, terribly sorry to have missed us. Maybe next time.

Well, now we are gonna make it up to them. Hello, Pacific. And good-bye to everything I've ever known before.

Among the things waiting for us in the port of San Diego is mail. My name, printed in Susan's big, strong handwriting, brings a smile to my face before I even open the letter.

Merry Christmas, Hank!

WAS I your first Christmas greeting? Yes, I was. And I will tell you why I was. And you take note. I was first because I am in charge. Well, I am in charge of a lot of things since you two sorry excuses up and left us. But most important, I am in charge of all post office runs around here. Why that matters right now is that I wanted to be first and I was not going to let anything or anybody get in the way of that. This is the part where you need to take note. See, Mam wrote you a Christmas greeting before I did. And she told me to mail it down at the P.O. Which I will do, of course, because I always do what I am told. But I also always do what I need to do to get what I want. Nothing can get in the way, Hank. You know? Nothing. So, I took Mam's Christmas greeting, but I held on to it. Then I wrote mine, which is this that you are holding in your hands right this minute. I will mail this letter to you now, today. Then in a couple of days I'll mail Mam's.

See? It worked. So, Merry Christmas, sailor! Now follow my example and do whatever you need to do, no matter what or who is in your way.

BE STRONG, be determined. BE IN charge. BE ruthless.

HAVE you killed ANYbody yet, HANK? I do not mean to be a ghoul or nothing, but I need to keep on this subject. everybody understands that you have to kill people in a situation like the one you are in. So do not be shy about that, as nobody will think any the lesser of you if you kill maybe a lot of people. We read that story, "A Christmas Carol," by Charles Dickens in class, you know, for the season and all. And I know it has that dead fellow coming back with his chains and how he haunts Mr. Scrooge in the night and makes his life intolerable. But I don't believe that happens really. I don't think anybody comes back and bothers you after they are dead even if you killed them yourself. I do not know if that kind of thinking was troubling you, but if it was, you can stop now. Kill everybody you need to, and if you are in any way unsure, then err on the side of caution and kill them just to be safe. Control your world around you as much as you can, like I do. It does not make you a bad person to kill lots of bad people. It does not make you a bad Christian.

*Have you heard from Theo?*

*You cannot really see it, but that space was a pause right there, Hank. It was because I tried to write, but I could not. So I left you the pause because you will understand me.*

*My heart is so broken I cannot stand it. I cannot believe it and I cannot stand it. It breaks every day again and I have to tell somebody but nobody at home and nobody at school and I am sorry but it has to be you. I have to be strong here and I cannot say these things because I do not want to make it worse for anybody here. You can take it because you can take everything. Please, please do not tell Theo because I do not want to hurt him. I don't know if he can take it.*

*Merry Christmas. Be careful and be mean. Then come home.*

*Love,*

*Susan*

There is some staring into space for me, after that. I put the letter down and pick up another one and I stare some more. Then I smile again, thank goodness. Then I can't help but laugh a little laugh. Because while Susan may have every angle figured in her quest to control her world, there is no figuring the workings of the postal system or the crazy movements of the armed forces during wartime and how those two things ever manage to synchronize at all.

Mam's letter arrived at the same time as Suzie's. And they both arrived long after Christmas was just a sad, achy memory.

Dear Henry,

I hope you are well, and that you are able to enjoy at least some small joys of the holiday season. Your father and I send you all our love, and want you to know we are thinking of you and your brother every minute of every day. Our hands and knees are near to worn out from praying. But they will never wear out. Nor will our hearts.

I have reminded your sister to write to you, but she says she is frightfully busy and will get to it in due time. But that is just our Susan!

Keep your head down, son, and your spirit up. And we will see you again before the A's raise that pennant.

All our love,

Mam and Pop

It's fortunate that she knows me so well. If she had not dropped in that very funny joke about the A's right when she did that might have been the most depressing Christmas post ever. And she managed it without stretching the truth at all, since we will all surely be home long before the A's win any pennants.

"Does it bother you, when you think about it?"

"Don't start, Pappas," I say.

Pappas and I are sitting on either wing of an F4F Wildcat fighter plane, which itself sits in the middle of a pack of Wildcats on the flight deck of the *Yorktown*. The nose of the fuselage is between us, and we each have a propeller blade in front of us and one of the 'Cat's folded-up wings behind. To me, this is about the greatest fort any kid could ever build for himself. To Pappas, it's just a prime platform for jerkiness.

"What? I'm just trying to understand you people, that's all. Like if it ever gets you down, knowing that really you are all just here to serve *my* needs? Because it would bother me, frankly."

"I tell you what, flyboy, if you don't knock it off *I'm* gonna bother you. Frankly."

"So, then you are touchy about it. Understandable. I mean, you are the boat people, right? Joined the Navy, only to find when you got here that it was all about *us*."

He is right. He is exactly and completely right. On an aircraft carrier, at least, it is all about the pilots, the planes, the skies. The ocean is almost incidental, in a way.

"It is not all about you. Be quiet."

See, Pappas is a fighter pilot. You have to tell them to pipe down all the time.

"Enough about me," he says, "let's talk about me."

"Can't you just enjoy the view? Just look at the view, will ya?"

The view is awe-inspiring as we steam north across yet another massive swathe of ocean. We have delivered a load of Marines to reinforce troops on Samoa, and we are navigating chains of islands with names like Atafu and Tuvalu that I would have sworn were made up if I heard them six months ago. There are places here I'm pretty sure do not exist in the geography books in the schools of Accokeek. But the thing I never get over is the plain insane *vastness* I never knew was out here, and it makes me feel so stupid I'm ashamed of myself. How are we Americans supposed to lead the world now if we don't even know what world is out here?

But even that has to take a backseat to what's awing me at this moment. It's not the vastness that was always here, the wide-open spaces, or the massive chains of islands and atolls that pop up out of nowhere.

It's us.

We have sailed along our plotted path to our assignment, and that assignment is a rendezvous between our Task Force 17 and Admiral Bull Halsey's Task Force 8. It is amazing, even though it shouldn't be. I am a trained Navy man now, but this, the firepower and the steel and the sheer muscle, is shocking to me all the same. TF 8 lies before us with one aircraft carrier, three heavy cruisers, and no fewer than nine destroyers.

And their task force is only a few ships bigger than ours.

I feel stupid all over again. Because I don't understand how the world doesn't just roll over and give up when they see this coming. And by *this*, I mean *us*. I am a part of it, and that is a hard thing to comprehend. It must be what a captured animal experiences when it first sees itself in a mirror. Or maybe what it's like when one of the last of a rare breed of wild beast accidentally runs into another of its kind.

"You gotta admit," I say to Pappas, "that is an awesome sight."

Inspiring awe in a fighter pilot, however, is about as easy as drinking the Pacific.

"What, that?" he says, making a two-handed, dismissive gesture in the direction of the carrier USS *Enterprise,* its complement of warships, and the entire

Pacific Theater of Operations. "You call that a view? Let me tell you about views."

"Let you *not*, please," I say, pointing a heavy hand at his still-motoring mouth because with these boys being subtle means being ignored.

He laughs right into my pointing hand.

I do love these guys. Right away I found myself gravitating toward the flight crews. There is just something about them, a spirit, an energy, a humor that maybe comes from the air they breathe up there or maybe from something else, something danger-driven that I'd rather not think about.

My brother is breathing that air. He's in the sky half a world away and it occurs to me that he's got a lot more in common with these guys right now than he's got with me. That notion would have been unthinkable before, since there wouldn't have been any two guys anywhere with a more similar past, present, and future than Theo and me. But everything is thinkable now, whether we want to be thinking it or not. *Especially* if we don't want to be thinking it.

I believe Theo is in the air right now, preparing for missions in the European Theater.

"Okay, it really is something," Pappas finally allows, as the full majesty of Task Force 8 comes into view. "That's a lot of floating *pow* right there."

It is, and I cannot shake the spooked feeling I get, a sense that I am looking at our reflection. It is like rounding a corner and finding yourself there, seeing an angle of yourself that you were never meant to see.

And Pappas voices my next thought.

"And with us and them *together* . . . mercy, we'll be merciless."

Like with most things, Pappas hit that one right on the head.

The raids we conduct on the Japanese military installations scattered among the Gilbert and Marshall Islands are the first real live warfare I have ever seen, never mind participated in. It is as thrilling to me as my first at bats in organized baseball. And like baseball, warfare has held a new excitement every time I've been bumped up a level. Joining the Navy, going through training, learning skills of seafaring and combat — it all just got more exciting with every step. By the time I finished my training I was an expert in hundreds of types of explosives and flammable fuels — and an expert in how to keep them from exploding and inflaming in my own face and killing everybody around me. A certain feeling of power and control came with that knowledge.

Then I saw the bigger and bigger beasts of the fleet,

and could not help gasping every time, feeling small and overmatched every time, until I was stationed on the *Yorktown* and almost certainly let out a squawk that sounded either like *Accokeek!* or *I'm Mac the hick!* Either way, it achieved the same thing in accurately announcing me to the new wide world.

And now, this. All the firepower being unleashed has my heart pumping so hard that, when I see Pappas laughing up there in his cockpit, I can't help but think he's laughing his head off at the racket of my heartbeat in that last thumbs-up instant before I throw the flag and the catapult throws him, *zhoooop,* out along the flight deck, off the ship, and into the sky.

I'm not supposed to stare. I have been told this over and over again as I have, indeed, been caught staring. But as my friend scorches the sky in his F4F Wildcat, I stand there staring after him.

"McCallum!" the flight deck commander screams, and the only reason I can hear him is that he's about six inches from the side of my head.

"Yes, sir!" I scream back, scrambling out of the way. Pappas took off in the last of the fighters forming the Combat Air Patrol. The CAP acts as sort of the eyes of the operation, scouting out the lay of things and intercepting any incoming aircraft if it comes to that. Once they're airborne, there is no pause for breath before the dive-bombers, the Dauntlesses, are rolling up into position to launch just minutes behind them.

The flight deck looks and sounds like chaos as I skirt around behind the crews sending the bombers up. I scurry back down to the hangar deck to start preparing the third wave, the torpedo bombers known as Devastators.

It is like the whole of the war is happening on the deck just above us as men bellow and holler orders and engines roar like no beasts ever did in nature. I hear the screech and scorch of the Dauntlesses and their explosive tonnage slingshot out over the sea toward their targets.

We move the Devastators into position, and ride the elevators up to the deck to find the last of the Dauntlesses out there just beyond the ship's bow. We do it again, getting the dive-bombers lined up one by one, amid the smoke and the roar and the controlled mayhem of the deck where everybody seems to be running nutsy willy-nilly, but nobody bumps into anybody else because this is exactly what we have been trained to do. This is precision craziness, and we are good at it.

I stand again in position off to the side as my Devastator pals, Valentine, Wallace, and Frew, check and recheck their points before getting the final okay and, *schwooom*, they too are off like slingshot rocks, hurled in the direction of the Gilbert-Marshall Islands.

Nobody screams at me right away this time, because our squadrons are all airborne, so I have a few seconds to stare. But just a few.

It's misty and cloudy all over, and incredibly smoky over the flight deck, so there is not much to see anyway. Just the same, those islands out there are pure fascination to me. I would bet money that most of the play callers who are so concerned with them right now most likely had no use for them before this big ol' war started and will have no use for them again once it's over. They are tiny little military outposts for fighting a fight that's got nothing to do with them. Some of the islands've got nothing on them at all, except for either us or the Japanese.

Others, though, have got people on them. Lives and communities, some I suppose even smaller than Accokeek. Going their own way at their own pace, not unlike Accokeek.

But I can't be thinking about that. We've got bombing to do.

The flight deck is almost peaceful compared to the wildness of the scene when the planes were launching. We wait for word, as the fighters and bombers do the true dirty work out around the islands and we prepare for their return. There are over two thousand guys on the ship and even if we weren't attacking anybody, there would be enough to do just to keep the place running. I have been shifted from fire crew to laundry and back again in the time I've been on the *Yorktown*, but it's almost as if guys like me live a double life here. That kind of job, kitchen duty, bakery, supply, electrician's mate, cobbler, that kind of thing is the day job that fills the hours and keeps the city together. But the real thing, the thing that gets the blood pumping, that separates this life from anything else I'll ever know, that's the battle station assignment.

And that's what makes me an airedale. Anybody assigned to plane-handling duties on the flight deck is known as an airedale. Pushing the planes, pulling them, parking them, fueling them, cleaning them, stuffing chock blocks under their wheels to keep them from rolling over the side, securing them or releasing them, bringing them up from the hangar deck or getting them back down again. Everything you can think of that involves the routine care and movement of aircraft on a carrier is the job of an airedale.

Except flying them, of course.

Yes, it is also the name of a dog.

Yes, it is comparable to the batboys on a baseball team.

And yes, I am as proud as I can be to call myself an airedale.

"Throw a ball?" I say to one of my teammates as we sit in that small calm pocket between sending our boys out and bringing them back in.

"Again?" he says, suddenly grabbing a broom and sweeping invisible debris across the deck. "Always with you and the ball."

I don't even know the sailor's name. To be honest, I don't know a great many names here on the ship. They are all fine guys, and we are a team in the truest and most important sense of the term, and that's coming from a lifelong baseball man. But the very teamlike nature of the operation here, unlike in baseball, makes guys practically interchangeable. I am constantly looking up to find that the guy alongside of me is quite possibly not the guy who was there a few minutes ago. Function here is like a massive furious beehive, where everybody knows exactly what his own task is and you only know what the other guy's doing if he's doing it wrong.

"Please, Mac," the guy says. "The birds will be back any minute now, and I just want to relax for whatever few minutes I can before we got to go 'all hands' all over again."

"But that's what throwin' the ball is for: relaxing," I

say, bringing reason to the man. Sometimes I feel like my true calling is to carry the word of baseball like a missionary bringing faith to these remote islands.

"Not with you it's not, coach. You never shut up about it."

Well, I may not know exactly who he is, but I'd have to say he's got my number.

"I'll throw with ya, Mac," a guy behind me says as he snags the second mitt out from under my arm.

"Great," I say, before even seeing his face. He is walking away from me, toward the big control tower that is known as the island, and I've got no idea whether we've met. His greeting doesn't help me out since guys here will call you Mac if they don't know your name, and they'll call you Mac if they know your name is McCallum.

The only place to be even remotely safe throwing a ball when we are on high seas in high winds is tight alongside the island. In the right conditions here, I am pretty sure I could throw a ball two miles out into the ocean. That would only be fun once, though, and then we'd be left without a ball.

"In this wind you could probably hit that ball clean over Washington's house, far enough to break Jefferson's window," he shouts when he catches my first throw.

Ah, so he does know me.

Keane, that's his name. Good guy. Good worker. Good curveball.

We throw back and forth, hard, in the shadow of the big control tower. The island is the perfect synthesis of what we are about here. As the command center, it essentially combines the bridge of an oceangoing vessel with the air traffic control tower of an airfield.

Except that, really, there is no tower in the world that can genuinely control this air traffic.

*"All hands on deck! All hands on deck!"* the voice booms over the loudspeakers before Keane and I have even gotten loose.

The controlled chaos is back. I grab the gloves and ball and tuck them into the special compartment I use in emergencies, behind a bank of fire extinguishers.

Before I can even think of my next moves I'm making them, just like I was trained, just like everybody else. We had precious little advance notice of the squadrons' return, I realize, as I stand on the deck watching the Wildcats make that distinctive sharp banking turn right toward the ship.

I get a small thrill seeing this, but at the same time I get a chill. This seems to me just what an enemy attack on our ship would look like if those were Japanese planes. Once I get the thought, I cannot shake it, but the planes come in so fast it makes no difference.

Pappas's is the first plane in, and it looks fifty-fifty whether he's going to land the thing or completely destroy it. The wings tip, this way and then that, as he fights the vicious crosswinds trying to level himself out in time. I hear a couple of almighty hollers from other flight deck crew as the left wing scrapes the tip of the deck before the plane puts down roughly.

It whips past us, and the initial pack of airedales scrambles across the slick deck, scrambling after it.

The plane hops, skips a little sideways, then finally its tail hook grabs the arresting cable that is strung across the aft part of the flight deck, and just like a dog being yanked back by its master, the plane jerks forward, then up, then back until it thuds to a stop.

It's probably the most violent operation I've seen yet.

There is no time to dwell on it, though, because there is another plane twenty seconds behind it, and another one twenty seconds behind him. That's the way it will be until the entire raiding party is back on deck.

I am at the left landing wheel as my crew gets into position to manually escort the plane to the rear of the ship. There are cleats every five yards to tie down the aircraft that will be left on deck, like mooring small boats, but things are too crowded on deck, with too many crafts still to follow yet. So we are to guide this one all the way back to the hangar elevator.

First, I rush underneath to the tail hook. I feel the crazy pressure all around as the deck officer nearby screams at me to "Get that bird unhooked! Now!"

It feels like it takes thirty minutes and I expect the next plane to come crashing into us, and the next one, but suddenly the hook pops, and the plane is moving forward. The arresting barriers instantly snap down, allowing us to go aft, and just as quickly they are up again to catch the next plane.

I can hear tires screeching behind us, engines roaring, men roaring, as the same dance happens again and then again as we reach the elevator and descend to the hangar deck.

"Holy smokes!" I yell to Pappas as he pops the canopy and climbs out of the cockpit.

"Yeah," he says flatly, hopping down. The wings of his plane are already retracted and pointing skyward. The Wildcat is half its original width now, and looks like a great green hawk signaling a touchdown.

"What's the word?" I ask him, as we wedge the plane back into the tightest corner. "Success?"

"Yeah," he says. "Success is the word, I guess. Hard to see much of anything out there. Weather's not cooperating. Found our targets, though, and the boys were delivering some heavy ordnance, so that's good. Took some installations out, that's for sure."

"Whooo!" I shout.

"Woo-hoo!" another airedale howls.

"Yeah, woo-hoo, I suppose," Pappas says, a lot more subdued than usual as he slouches off toward the flight crew quarters.

Back at work on the top deck, it feels as if bringing the aircraft home is the most tension-filled and time-consuming part of the whole operation. Not a single plane seems to come in smoothly. They wobble, tilt, bang down too hard, and bounce over first one, then another arresting cable. One Devastator torpedo bomber bounces right over all the arresting cables and has to be stopped by the last-resort wire barriers that are thrown up like a giant bird-of-prey net trap. Three times I stand and watch as Dauntless dive-bombers are waved off at the very last second because of their dangerous approach, and they have to make the whole big circuit all over again.

But they eventually make it in. And the raids on the Japanese installations on the islands of Jaluit, Makin, and Mili are successful.

My first. It is my first participation in an honest-to-goodness attack, and we pull it off without a hitch. I just know in my bones this is the beginning of a rout.

\* \* \*

"You don't know what you're talking about, McCallum," Pappas says as he looks over the side, straight into the wind as we head north to Hawaii. Finally.

"What are you talking about?" I say, kind of defensively. "You guys were aces. Mission accomplished. Home for dinner."

"Can you even count, airedale?"

Airedale. As I said, I am very proud of my role in this thing, and on this ship. The name is a badge of honor, even if the pilots are a higher life-form with their own special privileges and dining rooms with silver service and the whole lot. I have formed some friendships with them, and that has involved some good-natured ribbing. Especially from Pappas, who will call me by my title and whistle for me to make the joke even plainer without ever making me feel inferior.

Then there's a way of saying it, makes a guy feel like a dog.

"I can count," I say, strong on the outside.

"Seven," he says.

"Pappas. I know something's bothering you. But are you actually going to make me count to seven, just to humiliate —"

"Seven fewer planes returned, Mac. Seven fewer than what you sent out. If you are going to send us out there, I should think you would make the effort to keep track of us."

Now the two of us stare off. We are on the hangar deck, right up at the nose of the ship. The wind is cutting in and down on us, making hard invisible shapes in the sandwich of the between-decks. His plane and the others are right at our backs. When I passed, I noticed that one propeller blade was as long as me, and I shook my head once again at the scale of everything. Could they actually be growing? In a way, I suppose.

"I'm sorry," I say.

"Hardly your doing," he says. "It was us. Seven, Mac. That should have been basic, that raid. It ain't gonna get any easier than what we had there in front of us today. In fact, it's gonna get harder. Lots and lots and lots harder."

I don't know why I was expecting a different story. I had no good reason to be looking for some fairy tale here.

"We're gonna be fine," I say firmly. "And we're gonna win."

He turns now, his back to the sea and the sky and all the many islands ahead of us. He turns and considers me.

"You remind me of my little brother," he says. "He's fourteen."

"And you remind me of my little brother," I say. "He's bombing the Nazis to pieces over in the other game. If you'd like, I can ask him if he'll come lend you a hand over here when he's done."

Pappas's eyes go wide at me in shock, then narrow in fury, then widen again. He'll need to make up his mind.

"Make up your mind, wouldja?" I say, putting up my fists.

He works on it, settles on one eye wide and one narrowed. He looks like a pirate now.

"You're right," he concedes. "We're gonna win."

"Uh-huh," I say. "And . . . we're gonna be fine."

He winces, then reverts to pirate face.

I would swim all the way, right now, just to talk to Theo, to hear him, see him, just to know.

"We should go throw the ball now, Mac. This is the part when you ask me to go throw the ball for a while, right?"

"It is," I say, shaking my head and laughing almost by accident. I practically run to get the mitts and the scarred-up ball.

## CHAPTER FOUR

# Seeing vs. Believing

**B**y the time we finally approach Pearl Harbor, the closest any of us aboard ship has come to real danger was when we were accidentally rammed by one of our own ships, the oiler *Kaskasia*. She was trying to refuel us far out at sea when the weather turned particularly rugged, and she banged into us before cutting the line and aborting the refueling operation. It was hardly the stuff you would tell your grandchildren someday.

My first in-person view of Pearl Harbor, however, is a different story entirely.

This is a formal and solemn occasion. Everyone on board the *Yorktown* is dressed in whites, and everyone not essential to the navigation of the ship is lined up at the rail on the flight deck. I'm embedded like an imposter among the fly guys who have become my friends. As we approach the island of Oahu and then drift along into the channel to Pearl Harbor, we see the people lined up on the beaches to cheer us. And cheer us they do, robustly, like we have already won some big important something, rather than just gotten started. I have heard, and felt, crowds cheering before, and I have been on the receiving end of those cheers in baseball parks all around the Delmarva Peninsula. But it would be shameful, wrong, and altogether misleading to claim that the experience approached this one in any meaningful way.

Baseball is important. Baseball, in a way I truly believe, is exactly what we are here fighting for. And yet, at the same time, this is the first time anything ever made me feel like baseball was . . . small.

It is a contradiction my brain is not prepared to work out. It is also probably not the last of those I have coming to me.

Suddenly, it's as if somebody switches off the human volume. The cheering from shore falls away and the silence on board almost muffles the sound of the carrier's great engines as we make the last stretch of the channel and come upon Ford Island.

By now everyone — everyone on board, everyone in America, everyone on planet Earth — has seen the gut-churning images of the bombing of Pearl Harbor. It's already one of those visuals that feels like it was burned into your brain before you were born, like the Statue of Liberty — only in this case it'd be an evil version where she's got filthy black smoke pouring out of her eyes and all her crown points.

But it's different, very, very, very different, when you come here and see it. If I had to count up the number of grown, fighting men who are crying all around me as we approach the tragedy of broken Battleship Row then I would be telling one great whopping tale out of school that I ain't gonna tell.

Never swing at a bad pitch. Know the strike zone, and never swing at a bad pitch.

How screwy is that right this minute? That I am thinking that exact thought with dry and clear and hard eyes as I stare at the USS *Oklahoma* lying on its side half submerged in water, at the *Nevada* which almost made it out of the harbor but sits there now, beached and bleeding oil, *still*, into beautiful Hawaiian waters. In fact, it looks like these muggings could have taken place two days ago rather than the two months it really was. The water everywhere still bobs with debris, and it is coated in the thick, greasy oil that is hemorrhaging right now out of the dead dreadnoughts. The hull of the *Utah* breaches the water and points sickly at the sky while the most famous casualty of them all, the *Arizona*, points every which way, broken in half from the explosions, her mast melted grotesquely at a forty-five-degree angle so that it looks like it's directing its last lunge at the murderous cowards, at the criminal madmen in charge in Japan.

*A date which will live in infamy.*

We all heard President Roosevelt say those words, all of us together, right here on this vessel.

We heard it. But now we see it. Infamy, indeed.

Never in my life have I felt so vulnerable, to see this tonnage, this might, this breathtaking power lying broken and brutalized before our eyes.

Never in my life have I felt so invincible, so right and righteous, so sure and angry and *certain* that vengeance will be mine and ours.

The contradictions will be coming in hot and heavy from now on, I see, like flak from the sky. So be it.

I know I am not supposed to feel that way. I know that vengeance is *His,* sayeth the Lord. But I'll be Christian when I get home, and in the meantime if the Lord gets angry enough to take vengeance on me then so be it, as long as I get mine in on those guys first.

Know the strike zone, and never swing at a bad pitch. The voice of Mr. Flintoff, my high school baseball coach in Accokeek, Maryland, United States of America, has all but seized the controls at the center of my brain. Good man, Mr. Flintoff, good baseball man and good American. Never steered me wrong once. I was a far better ballplayer when I left his care, and far more prepared for a lot of things, too, and that's a fact. And, while I do not understand right now why he's taken over, I am glad for it. I am glad for it as I find myself, almost uncontrollably, heading for the big anti-aircraft cannons mounted toward the rear of the deck. I don't know what my heart's intention is, and I don't know the first thing about operating the guns, but I have anger and hate rising too strong and too quick for anything good to come of it. I have never felt such a blind fury in my life.

I reach the guns at just the moment. Just the moment when we reach the far side of Ford Island, deeper into port, where there is a great bees' buzz of activity going on, oblivious to me, oblivious even to the big beast of the *Yorktown* easing down their alleyway.

I turn instinctively, turn to watch what everybody on board is already watching, and feel a completely different something as the silence at the rails turns to murmuring, then to shouting out, then to clapping, like the whole equation is reversed from when the people on shore saluted us. The whole ship is one big voice now as we cheer for the crews pierside, and the two repair ships hauling a great monster up from the sea. The feverish salvage crews do not even pause to acknowledge us. Every square inch of me goes prickly as I join in the saluters and we pass the bow, stenciled BB-44, that is coming up for air, being returned to life.

The battleship USS *California*. Sunk December 7, 1941.

Getting back into the game.

With all due respect to the good people of Hawaii who cheered us into port, and the dedicated fans in ballparks all around the Eastern Shore League, there has never been *anything* like the almighty noise we're making now.

There is something else waiting for me in Pearl Harbor.

HELLO, SAILOR,

So, I HAVE NOT SEEN ANY ACTION YET, HAVE YOU? IT'S BEEN KIND OF MADDENING THE WAY THEY ARE BRINGING US ALONG INCH BY INCH. SO FAR THE BEST WAY TO DESCRIBE OUR ASSIGNMENT IS: PREPARE TO PREPARE TO PREPARE TO GO TO WAR.

AS OF THE WRITING OF THIS LETTER, I AM PREPARED, BROTHER. AT LEAST I AM NO LONGER STILL IN A PLACE WHERE THE WAR ISN'T EVEN HAPPENING. MUCH AS I LOVE THE USA, IT WAS SUCH A RELIEF TO FINALLY MAKE TRACKS FOR THE WAR ZONE ITSELF. I AM NOW IN A PLACE THAT KNOWS THIS BUSINESS UP CLOSE AND INTIMATE, AND THAT IS GREAT BRITAIN. HANK, THIS PLACE HAS SEEN IT. I KNEW THEY'VE BEEN IN IT SINCE 1939, AND that they've been bombed since 1940, but honestly, I had no idea. There are some towns here that got hardly any kids in them at all because they were moved away from the bombings. Towns with no kids, Hank. Strange ain't even the word. Big cities and anyplace with a lot of manufacturing were pummeled by the Luftwaffe, and I know we saw news reels about this stuff, but holy cow you just have to see it to really believe it. And I have to admit that we (I mean Americans) ain't seen nothing.

The local population here, by the way, is only too happy to point that out. Very happy to see us, of course, but I'm getting a lot of, "So where you been all this time, mate?" And Brits coming up to us, making like they are begging, saying stuff like, "Give us a tank, Yank?" or "Oh, you're money in the bank, Yank." It's all in good spirit, but I'll tell you what, with the stuff they do with rhyming over here, if I had your name I'd change it back to Henry for the duration. And even that might not be entirely safe.

How are you? Killing enough enemy fighters to keep your little sister happy? Is it just me or is Susan a little scary? I got a letter from her last week and I couldn't sleep for two nights.

THINKING ABOUT THE WAR RELAXES ME AFTER I HEAR FROM HER. I FINALLY NODDED OFF BY COUNTING NAZI SOLDIERS JUMPING OVER BARBED WIRE FENCES.

THERE'S A GUY HERE, A PITCHER, PLAYED IVY LEAGUE COLLEGE BALL. HE TAUGHT ME HOW TO MAKE A GRENADE OUT OF BANDAGES AND SOAP AND SPICES. ALSO TAUGHT ME HOW TO THROW A SPITBALL. DID YOU CATCH THAT ONE? I THREW IT TO YOU ON THURSDAY.

I CAN'T SAY MUCH ABOUT WHAT I GOT COMING UP, COMBAT-WISE, BUT IT'S COMING, BOY. I'M TAKING CARE OF THINGS HERE IN THE WEST BY HEADING EAST. YOU'RE TAKING CARE OF THINGS IN THE EAST BY HEADING WEST. WE'LL KNOW THE WORLD IS RIGHT AGAIN WHEN WE MEET ON THE OTHER SIDE AND SHAKE HANDS. THEN WE'LL GO HOME AND PLAY SOME BALL, HUH?

THEO
P.S. YOU KNOW WHAT'S ALMOST HERE, RIGHT?

The answer is baseball, of course. Spring training; that's what's almost here. Who does he think he's dealing with that he can slip one like that by me? He's the one who can't handle the hard fastball in on the fists after he gets set up with the off-speed junk.

Have we gotten that far away from things already?

Theo, Theodore, Ted, Teddy Ballgame,

Spring training. You are lucky, and you know that you are lucky, to be on the other side of the world where I cannot quite reach to give you a cuff around the ear. What has the world come to when you think you need to tell ME about the baseball calendar? I am very sorry for Poland and Belgium and all the rest, but I fear this development might be the most unsettling aspect of the war yet.

Have you noticed how big the world is, by the way? It's like the farther we travel, the farther it expands out ahead of us. A kick in the head, ain't it, that we're finally getting a load of what the wide world is all about and it's all on account of our tearing it to ribbons.

Seeing it to believe it. I understand what you are saying, kid. I understand it all too well. I am writing to you from the one and only Pearl Harbor. Yup, the newspapers did it justice (seems like a funny kind of a word these days, huh?), but at the same time didn't even come close. I know, contradictions, huh? How many of those have you killed yet?

And yes, speaking of the sweet sis...If every country agreed to just send their schoolkids to fight it out, we'd all be home by now and every nation on

Earth would be going to spring training because baseball and Susanish would be the universal languages. There will be no more wars when baseball is global, I am certain of that.

But Pearl Harbor. It nearly killed me to see it, Theo, I tell you what. But then, it brought me back, too. I saw us coming back. More accurately, I saw the battleship California coming back. Coming right back up out of the ocean. I suppose a lot of folks think of the destruction of that day being all one way — down — but it's not so. Our ships are coming back, right this minute. The California, like I said, but then we heard about the others coming back from the dead. Plans are for most of the ships to be put into action. They cannot keep us down, no way no how.

And of course, the first one back in the game was the USS Maryland. How about that, boy? How about that? Is it possible to be shocked, and thrilled, and at the same time not the least bit surprised?

I guess some contradictions are not so bad.

Such as, keep your chin up and your head down, and yes we'll shake hands at the crossroads of the world eventually.

*Good luck, little brother.*

*Hank the Yank*

*P.S. Yes, of course I caught your spitball. I imme-diately washed it off in good abrasive salty ocean water. You tell your college boy pal that real ball-players don't need that kind of chicanery (and if he needs me to explain that word for him in my next letter I will be happy to oblige).*

We spend two solid months at sea once we leave Pearl Harbor.

I have never known anything like this. Never expected to, either. Other than the artificial and yet very real city of USS *Yorktown*, no solid land, none, is part of our lives, unless you count the small bodies of land we send our aircraft to attack. We have been try-ing to slow down the Japanese expansion across the Pacific with our raids on targets in New Guinea. But every time we get the feeling we are making progress on this front, we get reports of devastating setbacks as the Japanese capture Singapore and the Philippines.

Meanwhile, we play a lot of catch on the flight deck, and we eat up practically all the provisions on board. The Coral Sea is a lovely thing, but I am sick of spa-ghetti, sick of bright sunshine unbroken by any cover (unless you choose the cover of belowdecks and no exposure to the elements at all, which I do not), and sick of apprehension, as the ship buzzes with rumors of a big battle to come.

Finally, we are ordered into Tongatapu in the Tongan Islands, where we are to restock and reacquaint ourselves with an earth that does not gently sway beneath our feet. We pull into Nukualofa Harbor and have barely dropped anchor before I have gloves and ball in hand and am hightailing it to the nearby beach. I don't even take the time to drag somebody along with me. Maybe I'll find a local, and finally my missionary work will begin.

It feels strange, the ground under me that was so natural in my pre-Navy life.

But stranger still is the feeling I get from behind, rather than beneath me.

It's like I am the pied piper of baseball. We've come a long way from the first days, when I was driving guys mad with my need for throwing partners at every lull in the business of warfare. Now I already have half a team at my heel, gathered and eager, clearly feeling that same need for real life, for normalcy, for a physical expression greater and more positive and more *home* than life on an aircraft carrier on a search-and-destroy mission could ever provide.

And that adds up to The Great American Pastime.

"So," I say, my feet stuck in the sand and my nose in the air, "you've all seen the coming of the power and the glory —"

"Just gimme the glove, Mac," Pappas calls out, and the gang all burst out laughing. I laugh right along, happy as everybody else just to be free and loose.

In the gathering of mostly air wing personnel, with some deck hands and others I don't know, there are a couple extra gloves and balls. Somebody has been wise enough to bring a broom-handle bat, and he brings it right to me, extending his hand to introduce himself.

"Mess Attendant First Class Bradford," the man says, offering me a firm grip and a wide-open smile. "I heard you played some ball."

I offer him the same, and I have to admit, some immodesty to go along with it.

"Seaman Second Class McCallum," I say. "United States Navy and Federalsburg A's."

"Pffft," he says, half-stifling his laugh with his free hand.

"Excuse me?" I say, a little indignant and a lot shocked.

"Sorry," he says, taking his hand down from his face and squeezing my shoulder gently. "No disrespect

intended. Anywhere in pro ball is something. But . . .
you know . . . the *A's*."

Pappas is now right behind Bradford, and laughing
loud enough to drown out his plane's engine. There is
another flyer next to him, a hotshot Dauntless pilot
named Vejtasa who everybody knows as "Swede."
Swede is draped over Pappas's shoulder and laughing
just as hard.

"All right," I say, laughing but not feeling like it, "I
know the A's have lost some games. But hey, it's still pro
ball, and who else here can say they've been *there*?"

Bradford shyly raises his hand.

I am not in the habit of saying *excuse me*, because
I'm not in the habit of needing to. But today is obviously an exception.

"Excuse me?" I say to him.

"That's right. I was playing for the Newark Eagles
when I enlisted."

"Sorry," I say, "never heard of 'em."

"Negro Leagues?" he says, trying hard to help me
out with my ignorance.

They sound kind of familiar, but I am telling him
the truth when I repeat, "Never heard of 'em. Sorry."

He is not flustered by this. "Don't worry; you will,"
he says.

It may be a fine team he plays for, and a fine league, but I've never heard of them, and the truth is when you get as far as I got in the world of baseball — yes, even with the A's organization — and anybody makes less of that than they should, or makes more of themselves than they should, well, it can't be let go just like that.

"I wasn't worried," I say, smiling politely.

"Lllllet's plllllay ball!" Pappas calls out, rushing in and tugging me by the shirt.

It's not a game, really, more a thrown-together patchwork version. A smattering of guys fan out into a loose version of infielders and outfielders. A couple of them are wearing machinists' gloves, most are just bare-handed. The bat is from a pretty thick-handled ash push broom, but still, it's a broomstick.

I am left bare-handed as Smoak, a Dauntless tail gunner, swipes my gloves and the ball. He hands off a glove to Valentine, who is a bombardier on a Devastator crew. This is acceptable only because bombardiers and tail gunners are insane.

Smoak makes a little sand mound to pitch from, and Valentine throws his shirt down for home plate. He crouches behind it while Bradford steps into the batter's box.

I am standing near Pappas at the top of the diamond; we're somewhat like a pair of middle infielders.

Everybody is chattering baseball chatter: no batter, no batter, humm-baby. Pure nonsense.

Pure joy.

Smoak lobs one toward the plate, and baseball season has begun.

*Crrraaack!*

I turn, as everybody turns, to watch the flight of the ball, into the gap of what would be left-center field, probably two hundred feet on the fly, over everybody. It lands with a thump in the sand, more like a shot put than a baseball. Swede, playing center field but really just swanning around in the South Pacific sunshine, *hoot-hoots* as he chases down the ball and throws it back in.

"With a *broomstick*?" Pappas says, clapping. Then he turns to me, pointing. "Better watch out, McCallum. I'd be hearing footsteps if I were you. You ain't the only pro in town anymore."

"Ah, Pappas," I say, kind of snotty. I don't even like the sound of it myself, but I can't seem to help it. "The *Newark Eagles*? Yeah, I'm not worried, thanks."

"They could take the A's in a series, I bet."

If the A's only knew the grief they were causing me.

"Listen, even the A's — the *Federalsburg* A's, mind you — would mop the floor with any team in that league."

*Crrraaack!*

My prior training comes in handy as I whip around at the sound of wood contacting ball. Good thing, too, because I look just in time to duck below a screaming line drive that wishes to take my head off.

There is much more hooting from the outfield, and then the infield, and most of it seems to be directed at me. Shows you what these meatballs know, as the one who should be getting razzed is the rag-arm pitcher who is somehow managing to make a guy with a broom in his hands look like Joe DiMaggio.

"The kid wasn't lying," Pappas says as he takes the throw back in from Swede bare-handed.

"What do you mean, the kid wasn't lying?" I say, not that it should be any of my business whether the kid lies or steals or wrestles alligators with his hands tied behind his back. But since Pappas is leering and talking directly at me, it makes me less of a buttinski to be asking the question.

"Well, he said he was the best player on the ship."

"Oh, no he did not," I say, biting like a fool at the bait.

"Oh, yes he did," Pappas says, having the time of his life. He tosses the ball back to Smoak, who's having too much fun listening to us to bother catching the thing. It sails past him and rolls toward the shirt-plate.

These guys would perhaps have some knowledge that I wouldn't have access to. Because of the privileged life of the flyers. Not only do they get better pay, better quarters, and special "ready rooms" to prepare for battle while the rest of us swarm around the ship like the worker ants that we are. They also get, at all their meals, a kind of banquet service to which us regular folk are not entitled. They get silver service and top chow and all the trappings of high class, high society dining. Including getting waited on by the ship's colored crew members in white gloves. I hardly ever even see those guys, since they hardly ever even see the light of day.

"Oh, yeah," Pappas says, "we talk baseball at every meal, don't we, Aramis?" Pappas calls over me to the general direction of first base, where Aramis, the pilot of that same Devastator crew, is lurking.

"We sure do. Talk baseball a whole lot more than we talk food or naval matters, that's for sure. Your name comes up all the time, Mac."

That tears it.

I rudely break away from the conversation and stomp right up to Smoak. I have my hand out, like a manager coming out to relieve a pitcher when it's just not his day. He doesn't have the ball, so I turn to the catcher, Valentine, who also doesn't have it.

Bradford is standing there holding the broom handle in one hand and the ball in the other.

I raise my left hand, and he tosses me the ball.

"You'll want this back," Smoak says, offering me my glove.

"I won't be needing it," I say, again conjuring up a tone that makes me want to slap myself, but again unable to do anything about it.

I know this is gonna be easy, but at the same time I know I also have to make sure it *looks* effortless if I am going to quash this subject for good. So I go into a leisurely windup, rear back about halfway, then fire a straight medium fastball right toward the glove.

*Crrraaack!*

Right, there are other ways of making it look easy. I rear back a little farther.

*Crrraaaack!*

The whole island feels like it's shaking with the hoots and hollers and catcalls of my shipmates, and I realize I have dug myself into something now. I could have stayed on the ship and had more stability under my feet than this tremor allows, but that option has obviously sailed.

For his part, Bradford looks a little shy and apologetic, which is kind and decent of him and only adds greatly to my embarrassment.

As does the fact that Valentine behind the plate is trying now to help me out of this. He's putting down signs, one finger, two fingers, three fingers, to tell me whether to throw fastball or curve or changeup.

And after a few more pitches, hits being sprayed all over the place, I am desperate enough to start obeying.

And it starts working.

I am keeping Bradford off balance with the changes, and his hit rate goes down to every second pitch, then every third. I brush him back once, sending him down into the sand with a hard inside fastball. I stare at him and do not apologize because that is just baseball, sir, and if he truly knows anything about it then he understands. To his credit, he steps right back in there, crowds the plate even more — I have to admire that. I also have to drop him again, and I do.

He digs right back in, and I throw the curve that is called for.

*Craack!*

He whistles one straight back at me, as if he controlled the bullet with his mind. I just barely whip my glove hand — with no glove on it — up in front of my face before it beans me. I catch the ball and jack-knife straight backward as I do.

I lie on the ground for a few seconds and consider things.

I consider that my hand feels like it's been savaged with a cat-o'-nine-tails.

I consider that I am covered with as much sweat as any naval operation has caused me during my whole enlistment, including basic training. So much for making this look effortless.

I consider, finally, that my right shoulder is throbbing and feeling frayed inside, like I have been putting more mustard on the ball than at any time in my life. Ever.

"You all right, man?"

Bradford is standing over me, the sun haloing his head from behind. From the sound of things, nobody else could come and check on me because they are too debilitated from falling all over the place laughing.

"Of course I'm all right," I say. "That sun was just in my eyes real bad, keeping me from being able to get up. So, thanks for the screen there . . ."

"Happy to help," he says. "Shoulda been wearing the glove. How's your hand?"

"It's fine. I didn't need the glove. Nice catch anyway, you have to agree."

"I would," he says, "except . . ." He points off to his left, where the ball is lying in front of a howling Pappas, about twenty feet away.

"Oh," I say, looking at the slab of pink ham that is my glove hand. "I thought I had it. Guess it's gone a little numb."

Bradford reaches down and offers a hand. With my pitching hand I take it, and allow myself to be hauled upright.

"I have to admit," I say, "I didn't think you guys would be that good."

"It's okay," he says with the generosity of the clear victor, "I have to admit I thought you'd be a lot better."

I consider falling back down, but conclude that that won't make me look or feel any better.

I become aware of the guys throwing the ball around the horn all around us, laughing and shouting and just having fun, and I am reminded of how simple and great this is supposed to be. If it wasn't for the Bradford factor I never would have even bothered pitching.

This is, I remember now, a paradise situation in the middle of one worldwide horror.

"So, what are you, an outfielder?" I ask Bradford. "I'm guessing left field. You hit like a left fielder."

"Nah, man, I'm a pitcher."

I consider one more time dropping back into the sand.

"Really," I say. "Hitting like that? You're no pitcher, man."

He smiles, friendly and victorious all over again, and holds out the fat broomstick to me.

"This is actually kind of nice," I say, gripping the smooth handle of the bat, feeling the balance of it and noticing the unexpected contours of the wood.

"Thanks," he says with more pride than when he talked about his hitting. "I honed it myself. Down in the wood shop on fourth decks."

"Well now it makes more sense, anyway," I say, waggling the bat like a hitter, feeling it now, feeling it coming back to me as I head to the batter's box.

"Sure," he says. "Of course it does."

We take our positions. I dig in, Valentine crouches behind me, and Bradford goes into a long and fluid windup that makes him look a foot taller and with twice the wingspan.

Then he releases from his high-ish, three-quarters release point. I see the ball come out of his hand, and I pick up the spin of it, even in the sharp sunshine. Curveball. Beautiful.

The ball sails in toward me, and it seems he's repaying me for almost plunking him. He's taking back the inside of the plate, establishing himself, and I am about to bail out of the box and drop onto my rear end.

But, no need.

It is as mesmerizing a twelve-to-six-o'clock curveball

as I have ever been subjected to. First, it buckles my knees when I think it's coming for me, then it freezes me stiff as I watch it drift back, over and over into the strike zone, outside corner, right at the knees.

I cannot see myself, but I can feel it. If you took a flamingo, taped a bat in its hands, and buried its feet in the batter's box, you'd about have what I look like right now.

Judging from the roaring, hooting gaggle of ball-playing Navy jerks all around, I'd say I have the description about right.

"My shoulder hurts," I say, dropping the bat right there and walking back toward the ship. "I have letters I gotta write anyway."

And that's no lie, either. I have to write to Theo to get that spitball secret from his Ivy League pal.

We remain in port for a full week, eventually taking on over five hundred tons of supplies from the store ship *Bridge*. It is a real holiday for the *Yorktown* crew, more relaxed, quieter, slower as we have effectively just taken a seventh inning stretch right out of the war. I have acquired my land legs once again, as well as a passion for papaya, and a new regular throwing partner.

I hadn't intended to make a point of engaging with Bradford again after that day. I came away with injuries to my hand, my shoulder, and my pride, and I wasn't too hot to sign up for any more any time soon.

But he tracked me down. He came up to flight deck the very next day just as I was finishing up my cleaning duties. I was, as it happened, just thinking of throwing a ball around. And there he was, right in my path. I could hardly decline his offer of a little throwing as that would be rude and Mam didn't raise no rude boys. So, we threw that day on the deck in the perfect breezy sunny conditions.

And we threw the next day.

And we threw every day. He was uncanny, how he could just materialize, right place and time for us to throw down tools and pick up gloves and do our pro ballplayers' routine, getting down to the beach when we could and throwing aboard ship when we couldn't.

I now have a curveball that would terrorize the whole Eastern Shore League, making me think almost seriously that I might be reborn as a pitching prospect after this is all over.

"Wow," Bradford says after the ball lands with a satisfying pop in his glove, "you're a fast learner."

He still has this irritating habit of highlighting the very, very, very small teacher-pupil aspect of our dynamic. I can't tell if he's giving me the needle on purpose or just not noticing, but either way it's a highly effective go-to pitch when it comes to shrinking me just a little bit.

And I suppose there might be some who would feel that a little bit of shrinkage would do me some good.

And, as this is probably the only thing I could find to complain about after a week of throwing and catching and yakking with the guy, I suppose I can take it. Throwing with Bradford is the closest I've found yet to throwing with Theo. I can't think of any praise higher than that.

"Thanks, Coach," I say, as the ball snaps into my glove. We are down for one last visit to the beach before we leave Tongatapu today for good. "I think you might have given my career a fresh breath of life with these pitching tips. I could make it as a pitcher if I keep working at this all through my hitch."

Bradford does not respond to that. That is, he doesn't respond in words.

"Hey, what are you doing behind there? Are you . . . are you laughing at me behind that glove?"

"No, man, no, I would never do that. Who knows, maybe you're right. If you keep working at it, every day . . . ah, why not, maybe you could pitch. Certainly for the A's, anyway."

"Hey," I shout, but it's pretty good fun all the same, even if it's sadly misguided fun.

"Anyway," he says, more grim now, with the rhythm of our *pop-pop-pop* of throws falling natural and right beneath our words. "Back to the war now, I guess, huh?"

"Yeah," I say, feeling the reality crash right into the Tongan dream we are in now. I am already attached to the place, and sad to leave it behind, but duty calls, and that is what sustains us. "Just keep reminding yourself what it's all for, and that will see you through, come what may."

He nods, slowly and silently several times as he holds onto the ball, looking into the perfect white sand.

"Bradford?" I call.

He snaps to. He zips a hard throw to me with a quick release from right behind his ear, more like a catcher throwing out a base stealer than a pitcher. It almost catches me off guard, and the force of the throw bends my wrist back.

"What *is* it all for, McCallum?" He asks it so seriously I feel like I must come up with an equally serious and thoughtful response.

"What?" is what I come up with instead.

"You know what I'm asking. The war. You always seem so certain, so right-side-up about everything. Do you never question it, the whole good guys and bad guys way of looking at it? I mean, the Japanese obviously think *we're* the bad guys. Maybe we are. Do you never stop to consider the possibility that we are the bad guys?"

I have just thrown the ball back to him and stand, dumbfounded, with my arms limp at my sides.

"No," I say, never surer of any answer I have ever given. "Of course we're the good guys. I mean, of *course*."

He throws the ball back to me and that will be it for now. I take it and tuck it and start striding with purpose in Bradford's direction. He does the same toward me.

"Maybe it's not as simple as all-good versus all-bad."

We are standing about a foot apart, and five thousand miles apart.

"Yes," I say very clearly, "it is. It's exactly that simple."

"Well, that's very nice for you. But it's been my experience that nothing anywhere lays down all simple like that."

"But it does, if you let it. We are fighting for our way of life. For freedom and the future and the dream everybody in America has for themselves. For *baseball*, for heaven's sake. We're fighting for baseball, and surely you are a guy who can appreciate that."

I gather by the end of these words that Bradford is staring at me in a highly strange way. The look is a little bit comical, which is a slight improvement on the tension of a few seconds earlier but still unsettling.

"I can't even figure you all the way out, McCallum. If you really are so naive that you don't see the whole big picture or if you see it but don't care."

What he says there instantly sends my pulse racing with anger even though I'm not entirely sure what he means. This apparently registers on my face.

Bradford shakes his head no-no-no, and reaches his hand in my direction. I tense a little, but calm a bit when he places his palm flat on my chest.

"I don't think you don't care, man," he says. "So I guess I've answered my own question there and I'm happy to conclude that you're just an ol' dummo is all."

I stare down at his hand now, then back up into his eyes. "Was that the part where the conversation was supposedly taking a turn for the better?"

He keeps his hand there for a few more seconds, which reminds me again strongly of my brother, Theo, who would maybe do something I told him to do but would make sure it was only when *he* decided to.

Bradford decides to let his hand fall. "I'm sorry, man," he says. "Maybe I kind of unfairly singled you out. But the honest truth is I wanted to hear it, really wanted to listen to what somebody like you, white and fighting the same war off the same vessel, might think underneath it all."

"Fine," I say, though still a little foggy on what he wants to hear. "But you know, you see those air wing guys all the time. Ask them."

He nods a couple of times, reaches over and fishes the baseball right out of my glove, and starts tossing it up a foot or so in the air. It's a mind focuser, that play, and I know it well.

"Yeah. Well, there are some good fellas there, that's true, even if they're maybe a little crazy. But the thing is, mostly when I see them I'm in my white gloves. Understand? So, it's different. We talk, but only as far as a certain someplace. Then I cut off. I can't talk about all the underneath, with the people who know me in the white gloves."

Now we are getting somewhere, and the somewhere is my almost agreeing that he's right. I am a dummo. "I think I get you," I say tentatively.

He finally decides he requires teaching aids to get through to me. He reaches over, grabs my hand with the mitt still on it. He holds it up, holds up his own gloved hand, and punches them lightly into each other.

"I thought you were somebody I could talk to," he says, sincerely.

Now I finally feel like I did something wrong.

"I am, man," I say, holding my glove up against his. "I am, and you can."

I feel some of the tension — some of it — sail off on a Tongan breeze.

"Good," he says.

"Hey, see, I'm not untrainable," I add. "Brown glove good, white glove bad. Right? Right?"

He's back to scouring my face with a paint-stripper stare.

"You being a wise guy there, sailor?" he asks pointedly.

"Certainly not. Just being a dummo, sailor."


We take the slow route back to the *Yorktown* when it's nearing time to ship out. For as long as practical, we take the shoreline route, walking in the shallow water.

"See this, even this?" Bradford says after a long silence and puzzling me again.

"What this is this?" I ask.

"Here in the beautiful Kingdom of Tonga, I am welcome on any beach I can find. Back when we were in Hawaii — which, if I'm not mistaken is an actual state in my own country — I went to try out the famous Waikiki Beach. Got kicked right out of the water."

"Ah, that never happened," I say, kicking water hard and splashy like I can kick away bad thoughts.

"Of course it happened," he says, exasperated. "Police cars came, three of them, drove me and several of the other guys right out of there. Humiliating. Like *we* were the bad guys, like *we* were the enemy. Five serving members of the United States Navy!"

I am starting to really long for the ship now, for its order and its sense and its certainty.

"Y'know, Bradford, nothing personal, but maybe you shouldn't even be in the Navy. I mean, all things considered."

I am watching the lip of the South Pacific now, focusing hard on it and its splashings around my footsteps. Until I become aware of walking alone. I stop, turn, and see Bradford about twenty feet behind me and staring, fists on hips.

"Nothing personal?" he says just loud enough for me to still hear him over the waves' low hiss.

"Yeah. I mean, if so much is bothering you about the whole thing . . ."

"Listen," he says. "I wasn't drafted. I *joined* this thing, willingly, enthusiastically. Because while the idea of a good people on one side and a bad people on the other doesn't make sense to me, I do know a bad *thing* when I see one. And I know we are fighting a bad thing here."

"Great. Just like I did. Signed up to fight a very bad thing."

"Yes, but nobody told you you couldn't swim Waikiki. They didn't tell you you had to sleep at least four decks below topside, below the ammunitions storage. They did not tell you you could not be on the flight deck at all whenever anything having to do with the aircraft is going on."

We stare, while Bradford catches his breath, and I kind of hold mine.

"Unless," he adds, composing himself extra dramatically. "Unless, I am jumping to conclusions, which would be a terrible thing for me to do. Maybe they did tell you those things, McCallum, and I have been way out of line here. Did they tell you those things after you had signed up to fight for your country?"

Even a dummo could work out pretty quickly that that wasn't a real question.

## CHAPTER FIVE

# Play Ball

**B**y the time we have been at sea for one week after leaving Tonga, there is no mistaking it. Steaming west and northwest toward Australia and then New Guinea, Task Force 17 gets busier by the day. Our aircraft and those of the *Lexington* are flying missions almost constantly to sniff out the Japanese fleet wherever they might be in the Coral Sea. And sniff is the right word, because every sailor and flyboy on board can smell it, the fight coming to us.

Pappas and the guys came back from a bombing raid on Tulagi in the Solomon Islands both excited and disappointed. The Japanese had just recently taken Tulagi, the latest victim of their apparently unstoppable gobbling of every little island in the region. Our flyers seriously hurt the Japanese installation there, crippled a destroyer, and sank a few minesweepers, but it just didn't seem like enough, compared to how much flying our guys are having to do to get at them.

The sense, and the scuttlebutt around the ship lately,

is that the Japanese strategy is to set up these installations on little dots of places that add up to one big road map leading to Australia, most likely through New Guinea.

Bases on the Solomon Islands and New Guinea are the only Allied posts left standing between Australia and the Island of Japan itself.

Australia's our one big ally in the region, and if the Japanese successfully invade there, our problems are gonna get a whole lot worse. The Japanese have been terrors enough, operating from a bunch of tiny island outposts.

Australia would make one mighty grand central outpost. And even if they didn't occupy the whole country, they could just isolate it. Big Australia would no longer be in it, no longer with *us*.

Which is what brings us to the Coral Sea, standing with our allies for the big fight.

The fight. As busy as we have been — busy patrolling, escorting, delivering, scouting, and of course sending our planes out on search-and-destroy raids to installations on the hundreds and hundreds of tiny islands dotting this vast ocean — we still haven't been in a *fight*. Not an honest-to-goodness, back-and-forth slugfest with real danger at stake for everybody on both sides and not just the flyers.

My stomach is medicine-ball tight, like I have never felt before. They haven't even briefed us on what's imminent yet, but it hardly matters. Everybody on board is going about their business as if it is business as usual. But I see. Most of the guys look just exactly the way I feel.

It suddenly occurs to me how tiny our gigantic ship is, in this endless wide water.

"Wanna throw?" Bradford says, making me jump like a cat away from a water pistol.

"Jeez, Bradford!" I snap. "Just throw me over the side, why dontcha?"

"Don't think it didn't cross my mind. Nothing personal, of course, but you just looked like such a sitting duck."

I had been sitting at the rail, on the hangar deck, staring alternately at the horizon and at the sheet of notepaper flattened smooth on the deck in front of me. It had been folded and flattened and folded and flattened enough times already that I was either going to have to think about starting over on a less battered sheet or else just send it in its current state. Though sending only "Dear Susan" would certainly get me in a lot more trouble than sending nothing at all.

All week. I try, and I fail, and I fold, and back in the pocket it goes.

Seems the closer I get to *it*, the harder I find it to write the things my loved ones need to read. Funny how much easier it is to talk a good game, when the game itself is still way, way, way over that way.

"I *said*, would you like to throw?" Bradford says to my apparent lifelessness.

I stand up, tuck away the sheet again, and lean out over the rail where I can see our partner the *Lexington* in the far distance off our port side. Our Task Force 17 has only been joined by their Task Force 11 for a few days, but I've already come to love the *Lexington*. For being there, basically. It's definitely the junior partner to the mighty *Yorktown*, but just the same. It's like the little brother who makes you feel stronger than you were. Even though you are still the big brother, too.

"Naturally," I say to him, holding out my hand for the glove.

"Naturally," he says, handing it over, with ball in webbing. "When the going gets tough . . ."

"The tough throw high and inside," I say, completing our chant.

Bradford leads the way and we are about to ascend to the flight deck when it occurs to me.

I pull lightly at the back of his shirt, just enough tension to stop his progress.

"What *are* you doing, McCallum?" he says without turning to face me.

"There's a lot of activity up there today," I say.

"Not that much. I can tell from the sound."

He's probably right. But it's been constantly busy today with care and attention to our beloveds: the Dauntlesses, Devastators, and Wildcats. Still, enough space for a bit of a throw, that's true.

But I saw one steward screamed right off the deck this morning. And I hope I never see it again, and more to the point, I hope my friend never does.

"Probably room enough down here anyway," I say, knowing well what a sorry substitute the hangar deck is for the wide-open sky of the flight deck.

We are suspended in this awkward motionless back-dance for several uncomfortable seconds before we are brought back to life by a far noisier intervention.

The announcement from the bridge, over the Tannoy, is unmistakable and unignorable:

*"Enemy aircraft approaching one hundred miles!"*

That turns out to be enough to get me to let go of Bradford's shirt. It is also just enough to get Bradford to spin in my direction and trade wide-eyed stares with me.

"I suppose you might be right," he says, "about it being a little too busy topside right now."

"Yeah," I say, lucky to even get that much out with what feels like a baseball lodged in my throat.

"*Enemy aircraft approaching ninety-five miles! Prepare for attack! All hands, battle stations! Prepare for attack!*"

Where we stand I need to go around him to get up to my station, and he needs to go around me to get down to his. As I make the first move to get past, he makes the second, to prevent me. He drops his glove and grabs my hand in a warm and fierce handshake, grabbing my wrist in his other hand.

"We'll throw later," I say.

"Yeah," he says. "Good luck on your battle station," he says, taking both gloves and heading down below.

"Good luck with yours," I say, running hard for the flight deck.

"Right," I hear him cackle. "Will you be wanting mustard or mayonnaise on that?"

Everything is going quadruple speed on the flight deck compared with whatever I have experienced up 'til now. The engine roar is already so full-throated and beastly I feel like surrendering to our own planes. Guys are running every which way across the deck, and this is where all the million hours of training and drilling pays off because if every man doesn't do his job *precisely* and do it without smashing into the other guys, then everything comes crashing down.

I see Pappas at the controls of his Wildcat, in the lead group about to take off and he has got his game face on like never before. I wave in his direction as I sprint toward the second group, my assignment, the Dauntless dive-bombers. The screech is almighty as the first Wildcat burns up the runway and takes off. The second fighter in the CAP group slings into the air with Pappas at the controls — followed, in nothing flat, by the rest — and my unit is up.

Everybody is shouting something as all of us airedales put our muscle behind lining each Dauntless in position at the flight line. Everybody's shouting something at somebody else while I for one am barely listening. We know this procedure by now like we know our own lungs, and we have to tell each other what to do as much as we have to tell the lungs, "in-out-in-out." I count on each of these guys to do his part just as surely as I count on my own organs.

One, then two Dauntlesses are in the air, and we line up ours. It all runs like superb machinery, just like always, and as I stand back I look up to see Valentine giving me a thumbs-up from the bomber just the instant before it's slung into the air. It all happens so quickly that the time-lapse between my seeing his thumb and getting mine in the air means I have given it to the next Dauntless in line, and barely manage that before it, too, is airborne.

*"Enemy aircraft at twenty minutes!"* the Tannoy belts out.

My crew is hustled out of the way as the Devastator torpedo-bomber group takes over the deck and somehow manages to speed things up even more. I find myself dumbstruck by this last bunch launching so fast, each bomber practically bumping right up into the tail of the one just out above the ocean in front of him.

"No time to be impressed!" the flight deck commander bellows at me. He points emphatically, like a third base coach waving me home, toward the battery of big guns just forward of amidships. "Ammo train, sailor! Now! Move, move, move!"

I am flight deck crew and would be satisfied to be nothing else, but the reality of carrier function is that you do whatever is needed at the very instant that need arises. We all know we can be drafted into the fire crew in an emergency, or plumber's assistant or, more often than not, somewhere in the chain of ammunition supply, like now. If somebody with stripes told me to take over the wheel I'd be right up there, though we sincerely hope it never comes to that.

I race to the guns as the streamlined flight crews get

to work on preparing already for the return of those same guys we just slingshotted into the sky. And it's strange to think that we have just launched our guys to find their guys, who have just launched at us. To think that our counterparts, the Japanese versions of the *Lexington* and *Yorktown* are out there, somewhere we can't quite see them.

The fighters we send out, however, can see each other.

Our fighters have intercepted the Japanese planes only a few miles out, and the battle is on, and it is fierce from the get-go. The sky fills quickly with their planes that have gotten through and our planes that are chasing them. The whole show is coming to play out right here in the skies around our task force.

Explosions are filling every sector of sky as the fighters fire constant barrages between them, and the ships of Task Forces 17 and 11 throw everything they've got into stopping the enemy aircraft from getting to us. In addition to the two carriers, we have a whole complement of cruisers and destroyers also unloading ordnance into the sky. I had never wondered before what it would be like to be inside a flaming, erupting volcano, and I'll never have to now.

My head is spinning in every direction at once as I come skidding to a stop beside the gun-mounting platform. I just have time to cover my ears as the five-inch, .38-caliber antiaircraft gun bangs off a shell in the direction of a Japanese dive-bomber a hundred yards off starboard. No sooner does that round go off before the gun platform is again geared up and churning for another one. It's a remarkable coordination of men and mechanism, with five different stations on the platform — mount captain, checker, trainer, sight setter, and pointer — all whirring away at cranks and dials and scopes to get it locked on target again and then, *boom,* it goes off once more before I can get my hands back over ears.

"Down below, sailor!" the rear man bellows while still doing his sighting job.

"Right," I say, "the commander sent me to assist with —"

"Down below!" he hollers, a lot less friendly and almost as loud as his gun. "Handling room," he calls at the very last second before it booms again, practically blowing me backward as I scurry away.

The handling room is just below the gun platform on the lower deck, and takes up not much more room than the gun itself. It's where the big .38 shells are stacked and moved and sent up to the waiting gun. The handling room in turn is stocked by the much bigger ammo magazine on the deck below it.

I scramble down to the handling room, and I'm pulled right in as if I'd been expected forever. There are three sailors in there already, sweaty and agitated, hauling the big heavy shells up and running them over to the mechanical hoister which then ships them up to the gun. The shells are like some great and lethal game fish that happens to be five feet long and made of brass.

"In here," one sailor says, sticking me into his spot in the rotation and now I see why. Blood is pouring all down his face and over the front of his white T-shirt from a gash that seems to stretch from the crease between his eyes to the outer edge of his left eyebrow. Once he's got me in position, he staggers right out of the room, hopefully toward the nearest medic.

"See that bloody head?" the guy in front of me says as he dumps his shell on the hoister and spins back toward the stockpile.

"Yeah?" I say, cradling my own big brass baby in my arms.

"You don't wanna play nosey-nosey with one of these," he says, tapping the nose of the shell.

"No, I don't," I say.

"And neither do I. So heads up."

"Right," I say, dumping my load and circling right back for more.

It's a very different version of the same battle down

here below. For one thing, the heat is oppressive, and knocking me out already in short order. I played a lot of steamy baseball all up and down the Shore, so I considered myself pretty good with the heat, but I never encountered anything like this before. And the weight of the shells themselves seems to be growing by about fifty percent with every third one I carry.

There is a satisfaction now, though, with every explosion I hear right above my head, from the explosives I literally had a hand in launching. Might be the heat, or the adrenaline, or a combustible blending of them and a whole lot else but right now I am seeing it, a direct line that runs from my hands right through to the big gun, to the firing, then yes, to whatever deserving target gets it right in the teeth. And I like it.

"You don't get anything done standing there staring at your hands," the other sailor says, giving me a shove from behind right into the stockpile. I was apparently holding up the line.

I get right back into the rhythm of the job, while at the same time focusing in on the battle above which I cannot see but sure can hear. And feel. I figure we must be doing well in the fight because I am certain I have not heard an unfamiliar plane's engine from anywhere threateningly close. I hear our guns banging away until they have almost become one glorious unbroken fluid explosion.

And, we haven't been hit.

This feels like it could go on forever, feeding this hungry beast. I have a whole new appreciation for all that goes on down belowdecks that I probably should have had before but did not. The two guys I'm working with show nothing that indicates they are nearly as taxed by this as I am, other than waterfalls of sweat and a growing chain-gang grunt song that I have joined in with before I even realize.

My grunting team spirit is altogether with them but my body near to heat collapse when I feel the slap on my shoulder after dropping what must be my hundredth shell into the hoister. I turn to see the injured man from earlier, smiling — I think — and stitched up. His wound is still weeping, but he seems otherwise refreshed by his break because in one smooth motion he shoves me out of the handling room and stomps his way to the waiting shell pile. I'm sure he takes at least the first trip with one under each arm.

It is almost a relief to find myself staggering back up toward the action on the flight deck.

Despite the remarkable improvement in the quality of the air, it's the wrong way to feel.

The first of our CAP fighters have landed already by the time I rejoin the flight crew. Teams are shuttling planes to the rear of the ship, where they are going to have to be elevatored back down to the hangar deck to make way for planes that will be coming in behind.

I stand just to the side of the landing strip as the next plane navigates vicious crosswinds, trying to steady the wings and get down on the deck. There is fortunately no more enemy aircraft around us and so no antiaircraft fire to make this any more dicey than it is, because the pilot just manages to tip one wing above the deck, just one second and one foot before he would have clipped it and torn the aircraft to pieces. A handful of airedales sprint along behind as the Wildcat skitters across the deck and is snagged by the tailhook before stopping abruptly.

I am up on the wing when the hatch opens to Pappas's very bloody nose gushing in all directions.

"Are you all right, man?" I shout, helping him out and getting myself covered in his blood.

"Unbelievable," he says, without any of the usual snap in his voice.

I help him down off the wing until he pushes me back angrily. The crew shuffles the plane away while another and another screech in just behind. I likewise shuttle Pappas finally out of harm's way.

"So, what'd you see, man?" I demand. "What did you do, who did you sink, what are we up against?"

"Nothing. I didn't see nothing but Jap fighters and bombers everywhere I looked. They just materialize, out of the air."

"What about their carriers? What've they got?"

"I wouldn't know," he says as our bombers start screeching in, practically running over our toes they are so close. "I never saw any of their vessels. We had all we could do just to contain what they were throwing at us. By the time we finally saw them off and tried to follow to the source, we were running low on fuel and ammo, disoriented, and they were calling us back."

"Oh," I say, sounding like a disappointed kid.

"Oh," he says, picking up on it and sticking his bloodied and exhausted face right into my relatively fresh and unbothered one. "Sorry to disappoint ya there, McCallum, but I'll tell you what I did see before we finally had to disengage. I saw some of *our* ships. All our good friends, on the *Neosho*? And the *Sims*?"

The *Neosho* is an oil tanker we have gotten to know well over recent days as they spent countless hours refueling us and other members of our force. The *Sims*, its escort destroyer, was there every step of the way.

"Yeah?" I say when he lets that hang in the air.

"Forget about 'em," he says, bitter and nasty beyond

what's necessary even if I had sounded maybe a little childish.

"Uh-huh," he says, giving me a backhanded smack near my collarbone that I hope was more serious than he had intended. "And *we* left them there. Arrived just a little too late, and departed just a little too early to stop the hyenas getting what they wanted." His voice drops. "We left them there, McCallum. *I* left them there. What am I here for, if I'm not here for them?"

He probably doesn't require an answer, but he shoves off before I could possibly provide anything anyway.

Between them, the two vessels carried over four hundred men.

Somehow the twenty-two hundred here on the City of *Yorktown* doesn't seem quite as unassailable as the first time I stepped aboard.

But I am still on the flight deck bringing planes in and clearing them away again when Valentine pops up out of his Dauntless, howling like a flying wolf that has won the whole war by itself.

"What?" I ask, newly excited for news that's better than what Pappas brought home.

He just grins like a madman at me, slaps one big paw on the back of my neck, and with the other holds up four triumphant claws.

"Four?" I say excitedly. "Four. Four what, Valentine?"

"One carrier and three heavy cruisers, my man, that's what."

"Whooo!" I holler, grab him by the flight suit, and shake him nutty all around. For his part he laughs and hollers back and jumps around celebrating right along with me.

"Calm down, boys," Smoak says, freshly sprung from his Devastator and seemingly in no mood to celebrate anything yet. "Four. Yes, correct, four. But you might want to add, it was the *wrong* four. And we only sunk *one*."

"Hey," Valentine shouts and makes a grab at Smoak. I find myself in the very unexpected position of trying to hold our own guys back from taking pieces out of each other. "There are no wrong kills here, as long as you kill them and not us."

"Can somebody please . . ." I say, and mightily shove them both at the same time in opposite directions.

"Reconnaissance was faulty," Smoak says, and is taking no pleasure in saying it. "They told us it was *them*, the big them, the heart of the large carrier fleet. Only when we got there we realized it was the second team, little fish, small potatoes. . . ."

"Yeah," Valentine says, "now that you've used up all your small-stuff comparisons . . ."

They charge like rams at one another again, and again I find myself practically throwing them the length of the deck in opposite directions. And, I am finding it shockingly easy to do so.

I think it's the rage. The rage at the thought of two Americans going at each other in this moment in this place in this situation. I bet I could throw the two of them halfway home right now if they try me just a little harder.

"But, a *carrier*!" I shout at them. "Sunk, right? At the bottom of the ocean right now, right? You got the carrier, right?"

"Right!" Valentine barks. "And Mac, I gotta tell ya, we bombed that thing to *powder*. Bombs, torpedoes, you never saw anything like it."

"Right," Smoak says. "True. It was the *Shoho*, I think, just a light carrier. Had, I think, like six aircraft on its —"

"A *carrier*!" I holler. "Right?"

I can be very persuasive when I try. Morale is critical in team sports, so I know when to try.

"Right!"

"Right!"

And we shout *"Right!"* back and forth at one another for long enough that it becomes just a sound but just the right sound, until there is no room for any other foolish nonsense, and when we have shouted it enough to be unable to shout it any more, we all head out, inside and belowdecks and away from the madness and the flight deck and the day, for now.

And away from the big fat floating thought that the big ones, the biggest fish, are still out there.

You wouldn't exactly call the night after our first real battle calm. We are instructed — well, commanded, emphatically — to be on our racks resting up whenever we are not specifically assigned to duty.

We're supposed to sleep?

Even if all the excitement is over, which it is clearly not, it would take at least a day and a half for my adrenaline levels and heartbeat to return to normal. So I lay there, awake.

I can't help having a thought I keep trying to push away because I know it's not healthy. The thought is, if this is what war, or at least what airborne/oceangoing warfare is like . . . I'll take it. Enemy birds came in harassing us and we lay there in our great mammoth steel hunting nest and simply shot at them. Like the

**111**

target games at the carnival. And then we slung our own aircraft into the bargain, and from where I sat, this was pretty much the way things should go.

It was almost fun.

I know better. I know better.

But I also know I am ready to compose a letter to my sister now.

Dear Susan,

Do you remember the time Theo and I took you to the carnival the year the Depression got so bad they became desperate enough to come to Accokeek? You were probably seven. Is that too far back to remember? Anyway, I know you know those shooting gallery games they have, where you just stay back behind the counter, cool and comfortable with your rifle and waiting for the ducks and turkeys and pigeons and all them to come sailing across your sight. Well, this, what I'm doing now, is just like that....

It's not a lie. It's a dream and a daydream, a fever maybe. But, not a lie, and certainly not wrong, to tell such a thing to a scared young girl so far away.

*         *         *

I must have managed sleep somehow because I am lying there, with Suzie's unfinished letter held flat to my chest when reality comes thundering back to life. Sirens blare all over the ship, guys are jumping up and bumping into each other, gearing up and running off.

*"Battle stations! Battle stations! All hands, all hands!"*

The scene on the flight deck looks like a complete replay of the previous day's action, which it should. If we have to run this same operation one hundred days in a row, then it had better look just like this one hundred times because that's what a fine Navy does. There is the added complication of much worse weather, high winds and sheets of rain coming down from very low cloud cover so things will be tougher still and so we will be, likewise, tougher still.

The Wildcats are scrambling again, and faster than ever. They practically tear the clothes right off your back as they scream off one by one, and I don't suppose I will ever see the sight and not feel my heart race like a jackrabbit.

The airedales are running hard all over and fighting with a slippery deck, but we move our planes into position like a hive of big noisy bees, and before any time has passed we are all standing there watching the breathtaking sight of our guys, in formation and filling the skies and without a doubt this time going to meet a date with something monumental.

We batten down and prepare for our part, whatever that may be.

I am packing away the wheel chocks, the rain still beating me from above and the roiling sea keeping me unsteady from below, when I feel a dull bumping in my side. I straighten up.

"Wanna throw?" Bradford says.

He's got two gloves with him, and they are already dark with absorbed rain.

"Are you insane?" I say, wondering that quite sincerely at this moment.

"Well," he says thoughtfully, "a good case could be made that I am, I suppose. But I'd say there are equally strong points that argue the other side."

I look at his defiantly cheerful smile and at the rain streaming down the whole front of him.

"Not equally strong, no," I say.

"Ha," he laughs, shoving one glove into my not-quite-waiting hands.

I tuck the glove under my arm, and look all around like a ridiculously guilty movie bad guy. But in a crazy kind of way this is a nearly perfect moment for a throw. The planes are up, the decks are cleared, and we are in standby mode. Despite the storm slapping us around pretty good, there is still an undeniable calm-before-the-storm sense to things now.

"It's not like we'll be in anybody's way," Bradford says, sweeping his hand across the largely quiet deck. Most of the airedales and other nonessential personnel have taken cover out of the weather to wait for what's next.

"Why not?" I say, and the two of us stride toward the semi-sheltered space in the shadow of the island, where all the officer types are undoubtedly huddled nice and cozy inside, above the deck and below the radar masts.

"Ball's awfully slick," he says, turning it around and around in his fingers.

It already feels kind of nuts to be doing this before we throw out the first pitch. But, as I stand across from Bradford, it really feels like the right thing to do, somehow important.

We are fighting this war for baseball, after all.

We both take small steps toward each other, breaking our rule of always throwing sixty feet, six inches, the distance from the rubber to the plate.

He nods, he winds up.

And a door crashes open at the base of the island.

"Just what do you think you are doing!" screams the flight deck commander as he stomps in Bradford's direction.

"Just throwin', sir," Bradford says.

"Are you two out of your minds?" he says, getting so close to Bradford's face that the *two* he's addressing must be Bradford's eyes.

I still feel invited to speak, though. "Sir, we were just trying to —"

"Do you know that you are not supposed to be on this deck, sailor?" he screams, making it clear I am not invited to speak after all. "Yes, you do. Do you people have any idea what we are facing? Do you? Are you aware what could happen at any minute?"

"Sir," I plead, finally getting him to turn in my direction. "I asked him to throw with me. Just to, you know, kill the time, relax, put our mind off it while we —"

"Your mind, sailor, is supposed to be *on it* at all times. Especially times of high alert. So you will not throw anything, and you will get that . . . *baseball* out of here and off my deck right this minute, before I . . ."

I am looking over his shoulder and at Bradford's expression and then at Bradford's body language, and his fluid, easy windup which I am always so envious of and I cannot believe it.

The deck commander is still looking at me when the ball sails past him and pops into my glove.

"Holy smokes," I say, as the commander spins back toward Bradford with such uncontrolled fury that he actually overshoots his mark, spins an extra half turn and slips sideways on the deck. He catches himself with one hand on the deck when the Tannoy cuts in.

*"All hands, all hands! Battle stations! Battle stations!"*

The whole ship breaks out in madness as every last body runs to his assignment. I throw the glove with the ball inside like a football to Bradford who tucks it and runs like a running back with it while giving me a big thumbs-up.

"Head down, pal!" he shouts.

"Will do," I call back, running toward the rear of the deck to help scramble our few remaining fighters to meet the skyful of Japanese Zeroes already plainly visible as they break beneath the cloud cover.

From the size of the air assault, this is the fight we have been waiting for. We knew from intercepted Japanese radio communications that they were planning their long-awaited assault on Port Moresby, at the southern end of New Guinea sometime soon. If this isn't evidence of their invasion force, then I'd hate to think what it might look like.

We are pushing all out to hurry the last Wildcats onto the flight path and into the fight. We are pushing so hard I believe we could get the planes in the air ourselves without any mechanical help.

The airedales are yapping all the way through it, too, like the good loyal seadogs we are. Yapping with the combination of excitement and fear that I know well because it's coursing through my whole self.

"Reports are this is a big force out there," the sailor beside me yells.

"How big is big?"

"Two sightings, two forces. Four carriers in all, maybe ten cruisers," he yells, getting louder as he goes along. Getting stronger, too, as his side of the plane gets ahead of mine and the thing veers left before I catch up.

"A battleship," he goes on, "destroyers everywhere . . ."

I lose contact with his words before he even finishes. The Wildcat is in place and we are waved aside and the thing is scorching the runway with our wet handprints still fresh on its tail.

I try to imagine what such a force looks like, gathered out there on the open sea. I've never even seen a Japanese aircraft carrier. And yet they are dominating my life.

All our antiaircraft firepower explodes into one

great symphony of armament as the Zeroes come within range of us.

And we come within range of them.

Machine-gun fire peppers the flight deck as planes bear down on us and zig every which way. I duck for cover as I hear both the whistle and the ping of rounds striking the rail and the deck within feet of me. Our fighters chase and duel their fighters and bombers, but their numbers are far too great for a fair fight. In baseball terms this is like if the opposing team were allowed to use a starting pitcher as well as an unlimited number of relievers. And, they were all allowed to pitch at the same time.

Then I hear it, the *it* we never want to hear. The unmistakable whistle of a bomb dropped from close range and the *boom* in the water a hundred yards to starboard. We are being bombed, for real. Even after all the training, it still comes as a shock when it comes, especially when it's not one of those sky-high bombers in the clouds, but these dive-bombing terrors which are pure airborne intimidation even when they're not dropping explosives.

*Bu-hoom.*

But another one does. And another one. I am clinging to the rail, alongside several other flight deck airedales who will all just stay put until told otherwise.

As I look, the sky is a crazy, streaky gray with thick clouds and bursts of smoke. I brace as I see one Japanese bomber start to bank in the midst of it all and swing straight back for our part of the ship. I could pull the rail right off with the tension, and then . . .

*Ratatatatatatatatata!*

They have him, oh boy, do they have him. One of our batteries of four .50-caliber machine guns has locked onto the plane and they are rabid, firing round after round into it and following the plane right down to its explosive smash into the sea.

Before I can get too deep in the trance of watching that one go down, a torpedo bomber comes almost straight at the front of the *Yorktown* and drops his lethal load into the water. He banks and flies off as the torpedo shoots through the water so close to our hull it creates a small wave and I brace for impact. It misses, somehow skirting along the whole length of the great ship and off to nowhere in the deep.

Our gunners are heroic, relentless and vicious, and I see several more Zeroes trailing smoke as they turn away.

Then, one of ours goes screaming straight out of the sky, barrel rolling, accelerating as if it can't wait to get to the bottom. It hits the water so fast we can see clearly as both wings snap off and the fuselage dives, then noses back up briefly with its bent backbone before going down for good.

Our small unit of CAP fighters, fearless and dogged, really isn't any match for the enemy air power. They tie up some of their fighters for a time but then the torpedo planes come in low, the bombers come down from above, and I have no idea how the bridge is managing to avoid it all while the gunners try to blast them all out of the sky.

Inevitably, we don't avoid them all.

*Boooom.*

There is a low but jarring thump into the forward hull somewhere below the water line as one of the bombs gets through. There is no immediate difference in the *Yorktown*'s performance as the guys with me at the rail exchange looks that are somewhere between what's-going-on and nice-knowin'-ya. After several seconds, the great ship appears to have shrugged it off. So we do, too.

It doesn't last. There is another bump, and another. I count at least three more torpedoes that come within a long fly ball of slamming us, and bombs that miss are starting to miss dangerously. They hit the water and explode with enough force that they still register up in the top deck.

"Repair party, repair party, repair party," the flight

deck commander yells as he comes along and taps several of us on the head like he's playing a game of duck-duck-airedale.

I stand to face him and he looks at me with an expression that says he is holding no ill will over the baseball issue. Or, possibly he doesn't recognize me at all.

He points frantically toward a swarm of sailors gathered around several officers who are organizing them into working parties. The bunch of us run straight over, hydroplaning across the slick deck surface until we bang into the backs of the guys already there.

They are assigning jobs based on nothing but need and speed and one officer points to me and barks, "Fire crew, third deck, go!"

I scramble, along with other assignees to other crews on other decks who will be patching various holes and dings and electrical foulings. The watertight door on the porthole we take to exit the flight deck is, in fact, slightly dislodged and not watertight at all.

I run hard all the way, passing frantic sailors doing the same in all different directions. Between top deck and second deck, I feel a substantial explosion rumble from down deep below us. On second deck I see one four-man crew hosing down some steaming and hissing machine-shop equipment. Suddenly it feels like everything is running at or beyond maximum output and once again I am made to see the million tiny weak spots that make the magnificent beautiful Fighting Lady something less than invincible.

I am breathless when I reach the fire crew on the third deck as they lay out and test all the firefighting apparatus in preparation for whatever need arises. Before I can even present myself, the officer in charge bellows, "Fire crew, *second* deck!" and even points straight up as if I am stupid enough to need directions.

I turn on my heel and run to where I am sure they are gathered, at the equipment store just next to the hangar area.

I see them, huddled in the relatively spacious hangar space, and this time the ensign in charge looks quite pleased to see me and starts windmilling his arm to bring me home quick.

I am nearly there, when an occurrence changes the game.

I hear the whistle, which is a different-sounding beast from the ordinary bombs, and a half second later, *bu-hoom . . . bu-hoom!* The almighty explosion somewhere behind me blasts me forward, right off my feet, and I am skidding across the deck surface toward the fire crew like a suicide squeeze as the *bu-hoom* follows *bu-hoom* follows *bu-hoom*, and I haven't even stopped skidding as I'm thinking that I didn't even get to send my letter to Suzie.

All the fire crew personnel have tumbled like giant bowling pins, and we all scramble to our feet as the entire ship and its personnel find a whole new gear of urgency.

The ensign grabs my arm as I am almost up. "Since you missed training, you stick by me and just do what I tell you."

"Yes, sir," I say, and the five of us do what normal common sense would have always told me not to do.

We run in the direction of a smoking, stinking fire hole.

The ensign, whose name is Wallace, has the headphones on to communicate with the Central Battle Station way down in the belly of the ship. The CBS coordinates all the repair parties and is in effect the nerve center. It turns out we got off lightly, as he tells us when he pulls off his headphones.

"Armor-piercing shell," says Wallace, whose tone and bearing suggests Annapolis to me. Which would make us practically neighbors in geography, though strangers in reality. "It's torn all the way down through five decks, exploding between four and five."

All of us make a gasp or a gut-punch sound as we continue with our simple task of hosing down every accessible inch of second deck. The bomb had not even exploded by the time it passed through here, but almost everything is smoldering. Between that, the various chemical smells, and something more biological and rotten that we start to scent as we get closer to the gaping hole itself, this simple task has its own nastiness built into it.

The action above has slowed down as the action below has stolen our focus. I squint into my work as I start to think of what damage has been done down there, and what it means to the ship. The boilers seem to be powering us on, but the amount of smoke flowing through the corridors suggests there is more than structural damage. We cannot see as well as we should because only temporary spot lighting has been provided while the electricians try and bring back the full electricity that was blown by this bomb or another. We peer down through the hole, and it is clear there are stores of flammable materials that are burning at least on the next two levels.

Wallace taps one of the other, more experienced firemen on the shoulder, puts him in charge of our straightforward job, and then taps me to follow him.

"We're checking in down below. Carry on as you are for the time being."

I actually get a chill as the lights suddenly snap on and we head down to third level.

We are barely through the bulkhead when the horror of what's happened starts to make itself clear.

The stink is noxious, assaulting us immediately. I have never experienced the like of it before. It's smoke, and it's burnt rubber and plastic, and I couldn't even say what all else.

Until I see it for myself.

It's burnt uniforms. And hair, skin, fingernails, everything else that makes up a member of the crew of the USS *Yorktown*.

"Central says somewhere up to thirty compartments took the hit," Wallace says from behind the hand that covers his nose and mouth. He is back on the 'phones again, listening, and could be talking to me or to nobody.

There is metal shrapnel sticking out of a steel bulkhead just before we get as close as we can to the compartment that housed the permanent complement of Repair Party 5, an engineering outfit. Medics and volunteers are laying their bodies out side by side by side by side on the deck in the corridor. I am doing doubly what Ensign Wallace did, cupping both my hands as hard as I can over my mouth and nose, trying to stop any more of what is seeping into me . . . and trying to keep all of my insides, inside.

Then, it fails.

My solar plexus spasms, and I jackknife as if somebody's hit me with a flying tackle. I keep fighting pointlessly as vomit and bile foam right up into my mouth, then back down, then up with twice the force, through my teeth, into my hands, out of my hands, everywhere.

"Come on, kid," Ensign Wallace says, leaning over and putting an arm across my back. He straightens me up, and I see the corpsmen going about their grim business, unfazed by my reaction. I see the row of dead sailors along the floor and again have to cover my mouth as I think about who they might be, might have been a short while ago. I try to look past them, along the corridor when I realize that's the mess just beyond Repair Party 5 — the mess, where the porters and stewards have been spending all of their time during this war we are waging.

I have no idea what damage is just beyond these good, dead men. I have no idea what other good, dead men might lie that way.

Ensign Wallace is surprisingly kind, and impressively unaffected by another man's vomit, as he walks me back down the corridor the way we came. He keeps an arm around me to keep me steady as he steers me back up to second deck. He's got the headphones on, and I look at his rapidly creasing face.

"Estimated fifty dead," he says, again in that strangely undirected tone of voice. "Many more wounded. Three boilers knocked out. One fuel tank burst by a separate explosion. Serious hazard there."

I am extremely glad I never sent my rotten lie of a letter to my sister.

But I won't be sending her a true one, either. Not now. Not after this.

I think maybe my life will be clocked by *after this*. Before this, and then after this.

This is war. This, is war.

We reach second deck and turn together toward where we left our crew on a worthy and healthy and straightforward assignment that could not begin to compare to other assignments going on. Wallace stops short, and slips the headphones down over his neck.

"No," he says, gently nudging me back in the direction of topside. "We have this covered. You should go back, where our guys will be landing soon, and where there's *air*."

He works up something like a smile for me there, but it's got so many inflections of other things I have never seen mixed up together before that it's more of a fright than a comfort. Though I appreciate his effort, and his understanding.

"We were neighbors," I say randomly.

"Huh?"

"Annapolis, right? Well, I'm Accokeek."

His expression grows a little more strained as he backs away toward his crew.

"I never went to Annapolis," he says, "and I certainly don't know what an Accokeek is. Topside, go now, get some air in you."


The initial impact hole is in the flight deck amidships, just a little aft of the island. I can see a crew already buzzing around it, working up some kind of temporary plate to block it up until assessments can determine a more permanent plan.

I can breathe better just by being topside, but my head is still swimming with everything and it may be my imagination or awful reality, but I am sure I smell gasoline and that acrid, horrendous singeing rot smell that I may not ever be able to outrun now.

The antiaircraft barrage has shut down and that, at least, is a blessing. I am fairly wobbly as I work my way toward the familiar loose configuration of airedale pit crews waiting for our masters' return. The weather remains bad, but less bad, the sheets of rain having diminished to irregular smatterings. Winds are troublesome still and cloud cover heavy, which is combining with the fading day to make visibility problematic.

We are all doing the same thing as we wait, staring up at the sky, focusing on the routine unknowables of the weather. We look like a bunch of shaky little ball boys at a tennis match.

I'm thinking about tennis now. I'm thinking about Don Budge. I'm thinking about my pop. I'm thinking about Pop and his saying about Don Budge, great Scotsman sportsman. I'm thinking about Pop, *right now*, as finally we see the first of the returning planes make a big looping turn in the direction of this home away from home that must be looking good to them by now.

Let's hope they forgive what we let happen to it in their absence.

The four planes fly in formation, then align in a single column as they make their approach in the low, difficult light. The deck crew all scurry into position, the signalman trying to guide them in. The lead plane waffles in a sudden gust of cross draft, his left wing tipping up high from the thrust of it, and as the pilot wrestles it back the other way at about fifty feet from the touch point, the whole operation blows up spectacularly.

The shock is enormous as our massive 75-millimeter cannons explode into action, their brutal shells sailing straight over our heads in the direction of the landing planes. The machine guns and then the 20-millimeter guns pile in and we see as the four planes abort and soar off our starboard bow that they are *Japanese* aircrafts. Every possible explosive we can muster follows the rotten evil killers as they hightail it into the gloom of the evening and I know that every last man has to be thinking what I am thinking: that if there was any true justice then the pathetic, confused pilots would have been allowed to remain lost for just a few seconds more. I would personally lead them on the tour.

As we resume our watch for our boys' return, the weather starts cooperating some. The clouds rise and thin out, giving a strange and disorientating sensation of the day running in reverse. Visibility is a lot better, which will be welcome news to the pilots trying to lay wheels on deck.

But there is another, less happy result.

One by one, my shipmates start rushing to the rail on the starboard side. I join them in taking in the grandest and saddest sight yet.

The *Lexington* has not had a good time of it. She has, in fact, had a spectacularly bad time. Smoke is billowing out of her, rising in columns into the sky as if she were not a warship but a floating steel mill. Even from our distance of a quarter mile, it is evident that this is not something likely to be undone. Smaller vessels are pulling up alongside the big bulky carrier, there to rescue crew.

The abandon ship order has already been given.

There are no words as we watch this gargantuan death scene across the water. The *Lexington*, a hulking, heavier vessel than the more nimble *Yorktown*, would not have dodged half the torpedoes we had today. The ship is listing badly before our eyes, like a great creature trying to lie down and die but unable to. We would not look away on our own, no matter how painful the sight, but for the fact that our guys, the real ones now, are swooping into view, and in need of us.

The pilots are with us finally, and the brutal day of battle behind us, as we gather together all along the starboard rail the length of the ship. The guys returned with tales of triumph, and a fair bit of loss. Thirty fewer planes came back than what we sent out. The big Japanese carrier *Shokaku* was hammered to the point of flaming uselessness, and the carrier *Zuikaku* lost so much of its air group that it is barely more than a floating parking lot now. The Australian naval group led by their heavy cruisers *Hobart* and *Australia*, left to hold the last line of defense before Port Moresby did exactly that. The invasion was defeated.

None of which matters at this precise moment.

We all watch, frozen, as one of our own destroyers, the *Phelps*, lines up in range of the dying ship's exposed flank. We all know why it's there. The *Lexington* has to be scuttled so that she cannot be cannibalized or seized by the enemy ghouls who would surely have her. *Phelps* is the unfortunate assassin assigned to the nightmarish task that every last one of us knows will haunt every last one of them forever.

There is a collective jolt up and down the rail as we hear the first blast, and a moment later the torpedo slams into the hull of the carrier. When the second shot blows through her side it becomes almost a physical hurt and I touch my own abdomen reflexively. It is unbearable, but we cannot look away as American Navy Destroyer DD-360 fires a third, fourth, and finally a fifth American torpedo into the body of American Aircraft Carrier CV-2, while every single crew member of American Aircraft Carrier CV-5 holds salute until she gives way and goes under the Coral Sea entirely.

It *still* took five torpedoes to make her go down.

*     *     *

The long day lingers longer, until we can do more death, for God or gods or the universe or whoever it is requiring it.

It is just after midnight when every weary but clean-scrubbed and presentable soul crowds up near to the port side of the bow of the ship and listens as the chaplain does his grim and sincere best.

"We commit them to you, oh Lord, back into your loving embrace," he repeats each time. Each time we send one more comrade down the slick purpose-built chute, each in his own brilliant Navy-white canvas bag. Everywhere you look, men are standing with arms draped across each other's shoulders and for once nothing else matters here in this population regarding rank or skill set, job designation or education, waist size, religion, or racial identification.

"You all right?" whispers Bradford, who is in my ear and across my shoulder and very much wholly intact.

I low-shush him and hope that counts as an answer.

It's like a kids' carnival slide, I think, as I watch one more and one more body go down it, except carnival attractions don't normally end in a traditional and noble burial at sea. That's what I am thinking as I make every effort to not think about the chaplain's words right now and as every splash gets magnified to five times as loud as the last.

## CHAPTER SIX

# Our Pearl

I would bet good money that if there are two words most likely to bring the greatest number of American citizens to both weep and gnash their teeth until they shattered like George Washington's window, those two words would be: Pearl Harbor.

So, the latest brain-bending contradiction comes up as my heart swells when the *Yorktown* steams to waters within sight of the legendary naval base for a return visit.

Our damage is extensive and well beyond the shoelace-and-chewing-gum level stuff we could achieve with our own onboard shop capabilities. The analysis had estimated that we need a full three months' intensive care to get us back up to full speed and strength for the fight.

However, the fight being what it is at this juncture, and the Navy being what it is at every juncture, the word has come down that the crack craftsmen at the world's most famous nautical facility are going to have to do better than that.

"Three *days*," Pappas howls as we navigate the narrow corridor to our destination. Just like before, locals are lined up everywhere we look, waving, yelling words that get lost in the engine noise but still retain all their warm wishes. If anything, the outpouring is even greater than last time as the people jump and flail to be sure we get it, because if there is anything more noble than a warrior heading to the good fight, it's one coming back from one with legendarily serious scarring.

"That's what they're saying," I tell him while returning the affection to one and all.

"This I gotta see," he says, waving and laughing. "I was frankly hoping for quite a bit longer here in paradise."

"Really?" I say. "I hope it's even less."

By the time we finally make it to Hawaii, seventeen days after beginning our slow crawl out of the Coral Sea, we already know what the internal damage is. Lighting systems are mangled on three decks and the radar and refrigeration systems knocked out completely. It turns out only six compartments have been destroyed entirely, while a couple dozen more are damaged. One fuel compartment was ruptured, causing us to trail an oil slick behind us ten miles long, and the gears on elevator number two are no longer functional. Five decks, of course, have gaping holes in them with various plat-forms planked over them to keep us from plummeting through during business as usual.

The fifteen guys seriously injured and in the sick bay have been making decent progress and will do better now in a proper hospital.

The condition of the fifty-two dead remains unchanged.

The morning after we arrive, the ship is coaxed into Dry Dock Number One and the water is drained out as quickly as possible so the hull can finally be properly examined.

The *Yorktown* personnel appear equally divided into thirds as the water is drained away. One third of the guys seem to be uninterested in what is happening anywhere but inside and topside of our mothership. They go about their business no differently than if we were out on the high seas. These are the hardened all-business guys who don't want anything else but to be back in the fight. One third takes the very different approach of wanting to use their precious free time to get away from all that, and these guys are fairly sprinting down from the ship and into every corner of Hawaii's holidaylands.

Then there are the guys in my third, who cannot move one way or the other without knowing what the doctors have to say about the Fighting Lady's battered belly.

We line up as near as we can along the edge of the dry dock when the inspection team goes down in their rubber wading boots before the water is even all gone. And everybody around knows just how huge this all is when we see the boss on that inspection team is the commander in chief of the entire Pacific Fleet himself, Admiral Nimitz.

"Okay, now I'm a little impressed," Pappas says. "A *little*." He pushes his way to the front of the crowd like a six-year-old angling to get Stan Musial's autograph.

Thinking that, I get a little pang. I've never even seen the kid, Musial, but *Stars and Stripes* says the rook could take the Cardinals all the way. I think they're a little overexcited there, but I sure would like a chance to see for myself.

"Admiral doesn't look happy," Valentine says as we watch Nimitz brush past the lead engineer to examine one of the burst seams on the hull. It's shocking, seeing just how much damage the ship has sucked up and played through.

"Think he's gonna shut us down?" Bradford says.

Smoak is, as usual, direct, certain, and more realistic than life. "Not a chance in the world, with what's coming. A carrier at this point is so valuable, if a blue whale poked his head out of one of them holes, Nimitz would just yell, '*Feed it, patch it, and float it. Now!*'"

Everybody's laughing at Smoak's Nimitz impression, at the gallows humor in there, at the fact that Nimitz is getting animated and loud at the same time, like a distant small shadow of his imitator. And laughing simply at the opportunity to laugh, nervous as it may be.

"Especially after the *Lex*," Valentine adds, and we all go quiet.

The inspection reaches its conclusion. Nimitz squares up to the lead engineer, who looks like he's being beaten with a teacher's yardstick as he absorbs the admiral's orders.

The final two words delivered by the commander in chief of the Pacific Fleet can probably be heard on every vessel in that fleet, in every cove of the Pacific:

"Three! Days!"

The engineer is still standing rigid, arms at his sides while Admiral Nimitz splashes away.

"Think we should go down there and help him out?" Bradford says.

"Nah," says Pappas, "he's just getting a little rest, while he can."

We hang there watching as the blood apparently starts circulating again around the poor guy's body and he starts barking and marching, pointing and organizing in just the way the boss surely expected him to. We haven't even cleared the area before dozens, and then hundreds, and then hundreds more workers of the famed Pearl Harbor shipyard descend and swarm all over the *Yorktown*. I don't know how they are going to get it done, but you can almost feel the old girl healing already.

Bradford and I start heading back up to the ship, when the three flyboys split off in the other direction, up island.

"Hey," Pappas calls, and we turn around. "What are you doing? Come with us, have a laugh."

I shrug, look at Bradford. "Whatcha think?"

"I think they mean you."

"What? No, Bradford, these guys are not like those people. Matter of fact, they're not like any people. That's why it'll be fun. We can observe the wild weird aviator bird out of its natural habitat."

He simply stares at me, somehow willing all expression out of his face. He looks suddenly like a much older guy. "I think they mean you."

I let out an exasperated sigh, then turn toward the other guys. "You mean both of us, right?"

Smoak jumps right on it. "Stay out of it, Mac. We were talking to *him*."

Bradford allows a few hundred of his face muscles to relax. Not that he's totally convinced.

"Nah, man, I was just gonna go back with my guys, help get things back in order in the mess, write some letters. Already done the tourist thing in this neighborhood, you know?"

I do know, as much as I can ever know. My plan was to do a lot of correspondence catch-up myself.

The industrial symphony of the repair operation kicks up as we stand there and it sounds horrific, like the ship is being attacked all over again but this time not a single shot misses.

"Ah, come on, man," I say. "Who knows when the next time we get liberty will be. And you don't want to be inside for *that* racket, do you?"

Bradford looks back up at the ship, then at me, then at our mad bombers awaiting a decision. He sighs loudly, and I slap him on both shoulders before dashing for the ship.

"Hey," he yells, "I thought we just —"

"We're not going anywhere without gloves and a ball," I say, running hard like I'm gonna make a shoestring catch to save the game and show that punky Musial how it's done.

*       *       *

Mostly what we do with our burst of freedom is be free with it. We do the primary thing we have been unable to do for the past several months spent almost exclusively aboard the ship: We walk.

It's a partly cloudy, warm, dry day in Oahu as we stroll through on the way into town. The five of us just walk and yap stupidities at each other as our legs get re-accustomed to what they were built for. We do the first mile in about fifteen minutes, we are so energized by the exhilaration of it . . . and, okay, the competitiveness. We do the second mile in, all right, fifteen minutes.

The pace slackens a bit after that, but it's still brisk.

"What's wrong, sailor?" Pappas says, taking the lead and walking backward to taunt me. "Conditioning a little less than it should be? You know, this is probably the reason you washed out of aviator training."

It's good when his head fills with the fumes of his own gassing because he gets sloppy. I smile indulgently but pick up my pace and time my move just right. I stretch out, manage to step firmly on his toes, and immediately he stumbles backward and falls flat on his back. I continue right on my way, stepping over and on him as I do. "Never went to aviator training," I say, and move along as one by one all the other guys make a show of kicking and stomping on him while he wallows on the ground yelping and laughing.

I do notice a surprising difference even since our last visit. The military, which was already a big presence here, seems to have practically taken over the place. We see soldiers and sailors everywhere, in every shop, restaurant, and snack bar that we pass. I wonder how I would feel, as a local, about the situation. The business people seem to be doing just fine out of it, and I'd hope the regular citizens would be thankful to us for being out there saving the world and all that.

All the baseball towns along the Eastern Shore were mighty pleased to see the opening of the season and sorry to see it go. I like to think there's a parallel there. We're a beloved traveling ball club.

Downtown in Honolulu, we pass a burger joint that smells so luscious that we cannot, physically, manage to pass it by.

"Oh," Valentine says, stopping right there in the middle of the sidewalk and spreading his arms out wide like he's going to fly right here and now. We all bump to a stop behind him. "Guys, while I love Lady *Yorktown* with all my heart, my stomach says this is going to be the meal that finally reminds us of the days when eating was something we did for pleasure."

"Hey," Bradford snaps.

"Sorry, compadre, no offense. But . . ."

"Yeah," Bradford says, suspended in the same glorious sirloin fog as the rest of us, "I smell what you mean."

"Smoak's buying," Pappas says happily.

"Oh, I am, am I?"

"Okay," Pappas says, "I'll split it with you, how's that? 'Cause, you know, it's only fair. I mean we make a lot more money than those guys. You guys do know, don't you, that we make a lot more money than you, right? You know, because we're so much more important than everybody who's not a flyer, right? Just makes sense."

Bradford and I just occupy space on the sidewalk, letting him get it out of his system since the facts are already well known and since likely the only reason he's reaching for his wallet at all is so that he can be a fathead and razz us with his little speech.

"Hey," Valentine snaps, "I make as much as you do, Pappas."

"Oh," he says, pretending to be all thoughtful about it. "You know, you're right, I'm sorry. Okay, you can pay."

"Wait," Valentine protests, "that's not what I —"

He's too late. Pappas has grabbed Bradford and me by the arms and starts marching off. "The works," he calls back. "Get us all the works. We'll meet you down there at the park."

"Hey," I say, while being towed along by Pappas, "I thought we were going inside."

"On a day like this?" Pappas scoffs, letting me go but still leading the way. "After all that time cooped up?"

Bradford sidles up alongside me. "I can't go into that place, dummo. Not allowed."

"What?" I say, already embarrassed. "That didn't look like —"

"Dummo. Maybe it's true, and pilots really are a lot smarter than airedales."

And that, of all things, is the part that has me snapping at the bait. "Who says that?" I demand. "Is that something you actually heard somebody saying, or did you just make it up right there to get me all riled up?"

"Shush now," Pappas says to me as we find a bench at the edge of a broad, lush green park. I remain standing with my arms folded while the two of them sit. In a really maddening tone, he adds, "Be a good boy and we'll get you a biscuit. You want a biscuit?"

Bradford splutters a laugh and nudges Pappas to do more.

"Right, you just have a laugh there, guys. But remember this moment, *pilot,* when your chocks aren't behind your wheels one day and you roll backward into the sea. You'll respect your airedale then, huh?"

I suppose I could be better under pressure, but my response wasn't so bad that the two of them should be staring at me silent and gape-mouthed like I'm some lunatic.

"Fine," I say, "I'm not sitting with you guys." And because I haven't lost this battle of wits comprehensively enough, and because this is the only available bench around, I just squat on the ground, on my haunches, in front of them.

Bradford leans forward. "Gimme your paw," he says with his hand out as the two of them crack all the way up with laughter.

I slap his hand away and almost make the mistake of defending my airedale dignity yet again when I stop short, looking at myself and realizing I *am* sitting like a dog.

"Pappas," Valentine says as he approaches with a bag of heaven. "That's terrible. Just because he makes so much less money is no reason to make him publicly beg for his food."

I don't even fight it now, as Smoak comes along and gallantly attempts to lift me up.

"Take the bench," Pappas says to them as he and Bradford scramble down to the grass to sit alongside me. "You have the riches, so you take the throne."

"That's more like it," Valentine says, and the two kings of the sky sit down and begin the process of bestowing the food.

I realize I *would* beg for this stuff right now. And the three of us keep inching up closer to it like we are doing just that. Good thing an airedale is too big a man to point it out to them.

The feast exceeds our slavering dreams. We dine on huge moist burgers with cheese and onions and some kind of sweet heady spice concoction that I cannot quite recognize but will always identify from now on as Hawaiian. These are teamed with full baseball scoops of potato salad and coleslaw and honest fountain drinks of root beer and orangeade and cream soda that are really carbonated and don't taste at all like flat water with flavored syrup. Great big sour pickles that crunch like snapping tree branches and make your eyes water are balanced at the end of the meal by creamy buttery fudge that does all the work for you while you just absorb it on your tongue.

We are very much like a pack of old dogs as we loll around on the grass, digesting the food and appreciating the soft island elements.

But I know as well as anyone that you can't expect flyboys to sit still for long.

"We going to the beach?" Valentine says, hopping to his feet to answer his own question. "We're already halfway to Waikiki, the walking's good, and we're all fueled up. What do we say?"

The flyboys are already on their feet when I turn to Bradford. "What do we say?" I say.

He jumps up. "I say I'd like another burger." He slaps his belly hard.

"Kitchen's closed," Smoak says, waving his wallet for emphasis.

"Then that just leaves the beach," Bradford says, and once more into formation we go, and onward.

My first impression, when we finish our long and taxing trek to Waikiki, is that it's just okay.

"This is it?" I ask Bradford as the other guys trot down toward the surf.

"This is it," he says, scanning every which way up and down the sands.

It is, of course, a fine beach, nice sand, great surf. But there are only sparse clumps of people around. Maybe because of the cloudiness that has settled. Maybe because it's about suppertime by the time we arrive. Maybe it's the war thing, and the barbed wire defenses I'm stunned to see all over the place when I shouldn't really be surprised at all.

Or maybe I've just developed a small prejudice against the place before I even came.

"Tongan beaches are a lot better than this," I snort.

Bradford smiles warmly and grabs the ball I've had snugly tucked in my glove the whole way. "You are a loyal dog, my friend. We gonna throw, or what?"

I head after him as he runs over the sand.

"We can throw, but this whole dog thing has gotta stop now, before it gets any more momentum. Stop that. I'm not trying to be funny."

The other three start exploring their way along the shoreline, toward the heavier defenses set up by a hotel.

Sixty feet, six inches.

Curveball, curveball, fastball.

The surf crashes with exactly the right rhythm. Precisely our rhythm, which just makes sense. Bradford and I don't talk at all because we don't need to. We sling that ball and grin and sling like we are as natural in where we are and what we're doing as the waves themselves.

" 'Scuse me, boys," says a deep syrupy voice that sounds like it is all wrong here.

I catch the ball and look up the beach to see two local police officers coming our way.

I hear Bradford let out something between a loud sigh and a soft growl.

"Yes, sir?" I say.

"Can I ask what you're doing?" the policeman says. The second one, bigger, seems to be the junior partner and just stands back being big. And staring at Bradford.

"Just playing some catch, sir, on your fine beach."

"I see. Where you from, son?"

"Accokeek," I say brightly, as if it were Brooklyn or Chicago or San Francisco and he'd start telling me about the great time he had there visiting his cousins.

"I mean your vessel. You are Navy, are you not?"

It's as if only the two of us are native speakers and authorized to do the talking, but I'm happy enough with that arrangement.

"You do know your business, officer."

"Well, I would, wouldn't I? Vessel?"

"The USS *Yorktown*," Bradford says with such raw pride that I wish he hadn't spoken up, but I'd love to hear it again.

The lead officer turns his head extra slowly in Bradford's direction and glares at him for some long,

long seconds. Then he turns back to me, silently look-ing me up and down. He takes a couple of long strides toward me. Then he shakes my hand hard.

"Everybody's talkin' about what you boys done," he says, possibly emotionally. "If y'all didn't hold that line . . ." He trails off, gathers himself. "I don't wanna be walkin' my beat here workin' for no Japs, is what I'm sayin'. You a pilot?"

He won't stop shaking my hand, until his partner nudges him and they exchange looks like it's the little brother asking for a lick of his ice cream.

I am shaking with the second hard squeezer when I respond to the first man. "No sir, but I do work on the flight deck. Sending them off and bringing them home." I look past him to where Bradford, on his own little island, is watching this with what might be fascination on his face, might be pre-sickness.

"Well, that's a vital job, too, no doubt about it. Thing is, though, that y'all probably aren't aware, but your friend here, he can't be on this beach."

"Oh," I say, trying to be fake-stupid but sounding more like the real thing. "Well, officer, we're only in port for three days, and then we are right back in the heat of it, probably worse than the Coral Sea from what the scuttlebutt says . . . and we just wanted to do a few special things with our very short time left. . . ."

"I was aware," Bradford blurts, and suddenly I am the one marooned on his own island.

"Did you say somethin'?" the policeman says, the two of them suddenly very interested in his thoughts.

"I did. I said I was aware of that rule of yours because I was put off this beach once before, and I took it. But that was before I went through all the things I went through as an American serviceman out there fighting for America. I was ten feet from getting personally destroyed by a five-hundred-pound bomb that killed fifty of my fellow American shipmates. And I carried one man in my arms like a baby 'til I got him to the medic, whereupon he died on the spot. And I still had that dead American all over me, little sheets of skin and hair ash and all that, when I went back and helped carry other dead Americans to the place of dignity and respect where we lined them up and cried all over them."

Bradford finally wavers a little there, catches his breath, takes too long doing it.

"So?" the policeman says, looking at his watch.

That gets Bradford his breath back.

"So," he says, sounding just respectful enough in spite of it all, "I decided then that I wasn't afraid of anything anymore. And I decided if any *American* ever wanted to put me off someplace where I have earned my place as much as any man alive, he was gonna have to work a lot harder to do it than last time."

It's good that I am not required to speak now, because I would not be capable.

"I see," the officer says through gritted teeth. "So, you a pilot or somethin'?"

The other policeman finally contributes to the conversation by donkey-laughing at that.

It is now a bald stare-down and I'm thinking we just better get out of here while we still can.

"I am," Pappas says, bouncing right past me toward the officer.

The policemen are stunned as the three flyboys come right up to them, shaking hands all around. "We all are, in fact," Valentine adds.

"Pffft," Smoak says, "you're a bombardier, don't get above yourself."

"You all fly from the *Yorktown*?" the officer gushes, and I marvel at how flyers can turn certain types of guys into bobby-soxers at a Frank Sinatra show.

"Yes, indeed," Pappas says. "We've seen it all, from above. Except what we haven't seen yet, which is gonna be even greater."

"Well, we all owe you guys a ton of thanks, we surely do."

"That's okay," Smoak says. "Don't worry about it."

Pappas seizes his moment. "Is everything okay?"

"Well, unfortunately, no, it's not. See one of your party has to get off the beach, now."

Pappas nods thoughtfully. "It's the airedale, isn't it? I begged these guys to leave him behind, but . . ."

"Seriously, though," the policeman says, his admiration for our efforts dimming by the second. "He has to go. Y'all can stay, but no, not him."

Pappas matches him by getting a lot less friendly. "Seriously, though. This is our crew. Proud and loyal men of the *Yorktown*, we go in together and we come out together."

"Well then, son, you'll need to go out together."

"We're not done using the beach yet."

"All right, I tried to be nice —"

"When was that?" Valentine blurts.

"You don't vacate, I'll have to arrest you all. Now, I would hate to do that, I really would. . . ."

"You mean, just the two of you?" Smoak asks, like it's really just information he's seeking.

"Right," the officer says angrily, motioning for his partner to head back up the beach. "Have it your way. If it's more police you want . . ."

"Okay then," Pappas calls as the guy stomps away, "go get those reinforcements. We'll wait right here 'til we're done using your pretty beach. If you still think you want to arrest five brand-new heroes before they can do any more hero stuff, and if you want to be in the papers when Admiral Nimitz himself comes to get us out of your jail, well, we are certainly guys who appreciate a sense of duty. . . ."

We all watch in silence, and in my case serious apprehension, as the two men walk all the way up to the road and get into their squad car. It is tense, no matter how much John Wayne Pappas swaggered through it, as they sit there for several minutes. I can't tell if they are radioing or not.

Then, they screech away from the curb, and we can finally let it out.

"Ahhhhh!" Smoak hollers at the sky.

I collapse into the sand and lie on my back, staring at the cloudy dusk.

"Victory," Valentine says. "Shot him right down out of the sky."

I turn my head to see Pappas and Bradford shaking hands like Churchill and Roosevelt. Then Pappas walks up and stands over my prostrate self.

"Did you like how I worked in that airedale bit? I do try to include you on everything."

I graciously ignore that and get right to the heart of it. "What are you, some kind of superhero or something, swooping in at the right time, winning the day?"

"Did I not tell you, McCallum? I'm a *fighter pilot.*"

I feel the sand give beneath my skull as I slowly shake my head at him.

"Yeah," I say, "I believe you mentioned that."

The remainder of our time using their pretty beach winds up being a sensational game of run-the-bases that goes on for well over an hour and includes take-out slides and tackles and everything. It's closer to football in style, and competitive as any game I've ever played in, and it only ends when we cannot possibly run one more pickle.

Then, exhaustion plus lapping waves plus all the events of the day and the month and the months before leave us lying all in a row in the sand, talking about glorious nothing. But I can't quite shake the memory of what Bradford had said before. The only one of us who spent any real time down there, at the very face of hell.

It is a brighter, clearer day we wake up to there on the beach. Bradford is up, sitting cross-legged along with Smoak as they stare at the sea. I climb to my feet, feeling strong after my best night's sleep in many months. I kick Pappas, who yanks Valentine's ear.

"We should get back," I say.

It is a hike, for sure, but we've all been through

those before. We are pretty well in formation and lock-step all the way, and it pays us back with increased energy.

We are a crew, a unit. And everybody who sees us knows it.

It's approaching lunchtime when we march up to our temporary address in Dry Dock Number One, and as unshockable as I figure we are by now, I am shocked.

Twenty-four hours.

They are flooding the dry dock. It's halfway full already. Which means they've finished with the hull. They are floating her already, for Pete's sake.

"Now I've seen everything," Valentine says as we all gawp like a bunch of yokels in the big city.

"Well, I'm pretty sure that's not true," Bradford says, "but this'll take some beating."

## CHAPTER SEVEN
# Dead in the Water

**W**hen we saw the *Yorktown* floating again, we knew it was game on.

There were two more days of internal repairs, but practically nobody left the ship. Everybody was a dogsbody, doing whatever bits of anything we could to get the vessel lean and mean and angry again.

As we pull out of the yard again, it's the most emotional departure I have experienced yet, despite every departure of every ship being emotional enough already. Every last shipyard worker, from all the shifts around the clock, crams the docksides to wave us out.

All one thousand, four hundred of them.

We can all feel the rush, like a blast of cool wind sending us out. They look and sound like an honest-to-goodness victory parade. Like we won the thing already.

How can we not, now?

We cannot lose, and I cannot wait for the real parade.

\*　　\*　　\*

The ship feels right as rain, strong and fearsome as ever. Maybe underpowered from three boilers still being at far less than full strength. Maybe dinged and dented and making some straining sounds that she didn't used to make. Still, I have absolute confidence as we steam north toward what the pilots are calling "our destiny," though pilots do tend to talk like that.

The reality is that to make the unmakeable time-table, the repair team had to do things a whole lot different from what they would normally do. There was no twenty-four-hour fuel drainoff before diving into the work, thus risking the biggest explosion of all time. The job overall required so much power the Hawaiian Electric Company had to arrange a series of strategically organized blackouts of the whole city of Honolulu. There was no individual repair job on each hull injury, but instead a massive steel plate was fixed over a whole bunch of them. The original top deck patch that was meant to just hold us together for a bit is going to have to hold together for a much longer bit because when I walk that familiar terrain, it is still there just as it was.

But, we're floating. And we're cruising.

Okay, fine, toward *our destiny.*

And by now, everybody knows what that is. And for once, the pilots might not have been a big bunch of overdramatic, exaggerating —

"Don't you *ever* have anything to do?" Pappas says, draping himself over me and nearly knocking us both over the rail and out of the game entirely.

"Well, I do now," I say, spinning around and holding my dukes up and threatening him in a most unthreatening way.

"Are ya nervous?" he asks, slapping my fists out of the way. He tugs at my shirt, and we start walking the perimeter of the ship. We seem to have picked up a walking habit.

"Me?" I ask. "I'm nervous for you guys more than anything. I figure the biggest hazard I'm gonna face is if one of you dopes smacks down on your landing and squashes me like a bug. And what are the chances of that, right?" I let that hang there briefly. "So, yeah, I guess I'm plenty nervous. You?"

He laughs his Errol Flynn fists-on-hips pirate laugh.

I let him proceed with it as far as he needs to.

"I'm gonna interpret that as a yes, then," I say.

"Oh yeah, out of my wits. But you know, at the same time, I *cannot wait* to get at this. No foolin'. I want this so bad, I swear I'm ready to just steal a plane and go ahead and start without you guys."

The *this* Pappas wants so bad, and that we are racing toward, is our rendezvous with the steel of the

Japanese fleet. US Intelligence intercepted a load of Imperial Navy communication that left no doubt about their plans. They are headed to our base at Midway Island, to smash it completely, take control, and at the same time draw us into a fight against long odds. By a stroke of luck, all our carriers had been out to sea at the time of the Pearl Harbor massacre, and they know they have to knock them out to completely dominate the Pacific Theater.

Midway Island, tiny dot in the great Pacific we now know so well, is so close you could think of it as essentially the westernmost of the Hawaiian Island chain. If we lose this, it more or less guarantees that from that moment on we will be fighting the Japanese from the state of California. We don't say impossible around here, ever, but if we did, then that situation would call for it.

"I think you should probably wait for the rest of the guys," I say seriously.

"Ya think?"

"Well, yes. Not that there's any doubt you could give them what-for all by yourself. But because when you left, the boys left behind would miss you so much, the loss of morale on board would be crippling."

He points at me like I'm really onto something.

"The ship would sink from sadness, you mean."

I realize he could go on like this forever if I don't abort.

"Yes, that's it. Fathead."

"Okay, then," he says as we round the stern of the ship, where a full CAP of beautiful, battered Wildcats sits at the ready. Without warning, he peels away to leave me strolling alone while he climbs aboard his beloved bird to personally recheck every last wire, switch, dial, and gauge for the six thousandth time.

"McCallum," he calls.

I turn to see him already sitting in the cockpit.

"What?" I call back.

"I like my plane," he says, and for all the world he looks like he believes he's saying something.

I wave to him, turn back into the wind and my walk and leave the two of them in perfect private peace.

Somewhere, somehow among it all, there has been a mail call. I find three letters on my rack when I go to my room for a few minutes' stretch.

The letters have posting dates from five and six weeks ago, from Theo, and Mam, and Susan. I have been dying for these, but also wondering what I will tell them when I have to respond.

I stare at the envelopes in my hand as I sit on the

edge of my bunk. One by one I examine them, tracing each distinctive lovely, sloppy version of handwriting that is so *them* to me, and that can bring me to choking up just looking at the letters regardless of what the words might say.

But the words will make it worse.

I can't think about this now. I can't look at even one of them, because I don't know what tomorrow brings and I cannot tell them a fairy story I know to be a lie and I cannot tell them a true one I know to be a heartache.

I open my foot locker and stow them there for when tomorrow or the next day or whichever day it is brings us glorious great news that I can bring to my people — the best, most deserving people.

The only reason this expedition makes any sense at all is because of the brilliance of our code breakers. If this had to be a straight-up fight right now there would be little reason for us to show up. The Japanese have the advantage in muscle, particularly with their four carriers. We can only claim to have two and a half, if we are being honest about the realistic capabilities of the *Yorktown* right now, and that is a substantial disadvantage.

If we hadn't knocked the carriers *Shokaku* and *Zuikaku* out of the game a month ago, even the element of surprise wouldn't be enough to carry us through.

As it is, we like our odds.

By the time we arrive at our appointed coordinates to the northeast of Midway Island, our carriers *Enterprise* and *Hornet* are in place waiting for us with their support vessels. We have all managed the stealth maneuver without the Japanese picking up on us, and that is our first major victory.

We steam to our respective positions to await the unsuspecting attack force. The *Yorktown*, the wounded warrior, is positioned on the outside edge of the force to let the more robust carriers lead the charge.

"You know who we're getting, don't you?" Bradford says as we spend our last moments of throwing sixty feet, six inches away from each other on the hangar deck.

"Oh, I know well who we're getting, my friend."

The Japanese strike force we're up against is built around four familiar players: the remaining aircraft carriers from the attack on Pearl Harbor. There is not a single man in the US Navy who has not dreamed about the chance to put *Kaga*, *Soryu*, *Hiryu*, and *Akagi* on the ocean floor. They are a frightening assembly of naval power by all accounts. But at the same time, we could not ask for any greater motivation.

As we are throwing, we are aware what is probably happening on Midway itself, and it's not a happy thought. We all know Japan's attack plan from the intercepted communications, but the success of our own strategy rides on our carriers remaining undetected and that means we cannot do a thing to help defend the island. In all likelihood those boys are absorbing some kind of horrific pounding by the meat of the carrier air groups.

We know it's happening, in fact, when the loud-speakers indicate the setup is playing out as planned.

*"All flight personnel, all flight deck crew, to your stations. To your stations now."*

Bradford throws me one last looping curve, and I marvel at the beauty of the thing once more. We close that sixty feet, six inch gap between us in a couple of seconds, and when I extend my hand to shake his, he pays no attention, walks right through it, and grabs me in a big, back-pounding hug. I hug him back.

"Kinda feels like the big day this time, huh?" he says.

"Kinda does," I say. And even though we are playing with my gloves today — no, mine and Theo's gloves — I give them to him to hold on to. "Not sure I can trust 'em up topside right now," I say when he gives me a quizzical look.

"They're safe with me, McCallum," he says as I start running for top deck.

"I know they are, Bradford."

They're safe, and they're together.

This is the most crazy the flight deck has ever been. There is one group of six CAP fighters, including Pappas, landing right now. We hustle through our routine, clearing these guys just in time to get the next group of six in the air. A wave of airedales rushes out to spot the deck for takeoff again, while my team tends to checking and refueling this group, prepping them to go right back up at no notice.

"It's madness out there, pal," Pappas says as I climb up on his wing. "Every plane Midway could possibly have was up there . . . and most of them went back down again. They're overwhelmed. If we don't do something soon, Midway will *be* Japanese before we even launch anything. The island was taking a pummeling right up until the attack force started peeling off back to their ships to refuel and rearm. We had to scramble so's not to give us away, but the runway was still ours last I saw."

As we speak, a squad of Devastator torpedo bombers rushes past us, lining up for immediate takeoff. The Dauntless dive-bombers are right behind them. The flight deck commander runs along shouting for us to get these Wildcats ready and right back in the flight line.

"Never seen anything like this before," I say.

"Neither have I," Pappas says, "and I've seen everything."

I smack him a whole bunch of times on his helmet. "Keep this thing from getting shot off, okay? Because there's not another one like it."

He smiles real hard and slaps my cheek. "That's very sweet. I mean, blindingly obvious, but sweet all the same." Then he starts bucking in his seat, like he's trying to force it into motion with his body.

"Right," I say, jumping off, disconnecting the fuel line so the other guys can shove him around into line.

I scurry back up deck to where the last two Devastators are waiting to go. I run up just in time to see Valentine's TBD just getting away. I catch sight of the side of his head, but he doesn't see me. I wave him off anyway.

It's all going so fast now that Smoak's tense expression is in front of me before I know it and he gives me a very nervous-looking thumbs-up. I match the thumbs-up, but add a confident smile to see him off.

They have decided to keep Pappas's CAP group waiting, in readiness for now. It has to be killing him, to be in the cockpit and at the cusp of the action but made to cool his heels. It is obvious now, that the targets have been located and the time deemed right for the strike. All we can do now here on deck is hope, make ready, make busy, be ready.

It's excruciating.

The flyers do all our attacking. I've still never seen a Japanese aircraft carrier with my own eyes.

But if it's maddening for me, I can't imagine what it's like for Pappas and the other five fighter pilots who are in suspended action, suspended time. They wait there for what feels like hours, not allowed to get out and not allowed to go up for reasons known only to the brass. Things must be changing so quickly out there that plans can go out of date before they can go into action. Because there was clearly a plan for these guys when they lined them up. Then, nothing. It gets a little more chilling with every minute they sit.

And then, just as quickly, they are sent. The deck coordinators have to practically hold each plane back with their own hands to keep them from climbing up each other's backs on takeoff. It's the quickest-succession six-plane launch I will ever see because it is simply impossible to bunch them any closer together. But they are up, and we can see right away that they are strictly pulling CAP duty, flying formations above the ship rather than joining any search for trouble.

I feel for Pappas, who is yearning for trouble.

It's another long wait for indicators. The *Yorktown* is, by design, the third player among this carrier force, so the planes of *Enterprise* and *Hornet* will be gaining all the knowledge out there first, then relaying it back to our guys. This is probably adding an extra layer of delay, of processing and adapting to the realities out on the leading edge. So we just need more patience, which is fine even if it's not.

The morning is burning away now and the day's feeling fat when we hear familiar engines and then see a number of our guys come out of the clouds and into view. The sky is gray and the visibility much better at lower levels, so their appearance is dramatic, almost theatrical, and causes a suitably excited frenzy on the deck as they approach.

Then, just as suddenly and just as dramatically, our squad of CAP fighters scorch off in the direction the bombers came in from.

They are not quite out of sight when the first and second Dauntlesses land. There are maybe a dozen more falling in behind them as my crew sees the first one off the line and over to refueling and rearming.

"Well?" I holler up to the guys as I work the fuel line into place. Several airedales hurry to attach fresh bombs underneath since all 2,250 pounds of external ordnance have been happily deployed.

The gunner flips up the hood on the rear cockpit and I'm thrilled to see Smoak's wild excited mug pop into view.

"We did it, Mac. Oh boy, did we do it. We caught 'em changing shifts. Loads of planes back from Midway, refueling and reloading. Decks absolutely loaded with bombs and torpedoes and fuel when we caught 'em with their pants around their ankles."

"*Boom, boom, boom, boom!*" the pilot says, popping his front cockpit hood. All around us the same scenes and the same screams, as mad-hatter Dauntless crews compete to tell it the loudest, the quickest. Eventually I have to focus on the fuel line and let it all sink in at once.

"Three carriers, they were all . . . doing this here, actually!" one of them hollers out, laughing.

I look up at Smoak, and I am panicking as I make the connection. We are right now at our absolute maximum vulnerability. A lit cigarette could practically wipe us out, and I want his face to reassure me, which it does for the moment.

"Three carriers, McCallum. We got em! *Soryu*, *Kaga*, *Akagi*. Three of the cowardly monsters from

Pearl Harbor. We did it! We got 'em back and then some. Beautiful. Beautiful. Took no more than five minutes, total, they were hit too many times to count. Smoke everywhere, fire everywhere."

"Wow," I say. "Wow-wow-wow!" I fill with an immense, overwhelming, and dizzying pride at being part of the team that finally paid them back for what they did. For what they did to everybody.

"Hurry it up, boys!" one of the other pilots yells. "Job ain't finished yet. There's one more out there and we're gonna hunt that dog down and give him just what the others got. Come on, you airedales!" All the crews whoop and holler, and we do our best to do it faster than humanly possible, as only airedales can.

We break records for sure as we get our Dauntlesses fighting fit again. We are lining them up now, and with Smoak in the third plane back itching at the trigger, I scan the skies, thinking about what's next.

Shouldn't we be crazy busy with returning heroes by now?

"Smoak?" I shout, as he snaps his cockpit glass hard into locking position.

He is busying himself at busying himself, checking his details all around the inside.

The planes are all revving and roaring together for

the takeoff, second one is gone, third is lined up. It's impossible for him to hear me, but I know he can feel my staring at him. I know it. I know it.

Just as they line up to jump, he looks my way. His lips are pulled tight and he goes into a spiral of nodding and shaking his head *no* that has me confused and concerned and suddenly completely disoriented. I am in a kind of trance as he takes off without my managing to raise a hand of *good luck* or *farewell* or *thanks, pal*.

I continue to watch as they tear up the sky on their way to hopefully tear up *Hiryu* and finally complete the set.

I become aware eventually of most of the other guys staring up at the sky, too, like a whole bunch of good dogs waiting for master's return.

It *sounds* like we have won already.

Why doesn't it feel like we have?


Not long after the last of the bombers are out of sight, we get surprise orders to bring up the last few Wildcats from the hangar deck, elevator them up, and prep them double time.

Now, for the first time, we have something close to true chaos on the *Yorktown*. Even when we were bombed on the Coral Sea, the sense of high anxiety I feel now never took hold. As we bring up the Wildcats, working twelve men to a plane to get it done, the dread is all over everybody's faces.

These planes were down one level for good reason. They were in various states of disrepair, and were not battle ready. One of them had crashed just this morning, and taken out two barriers that had to be repaired even while planes were taking off and landing within feet of them.

"That's enough, that's enough," the flight deck commander says, ripping the line right out of my hands and leaving it spewing fuel all over the deck. Just through sheer overstock of airedale power do we get this plane and then three others shoved up and off the front of the ship. One more comes limping up to the spot, and it is well past brave that the officer drafted to fly it has gotten it this far. But it dips alarmingly on takeoff, more like a glider than a powered fighter plane, and we all watch in horror as it fails to get any lift before dipping a wing and crashing violently into the water a quarter mile away.

We have mere seconds to work through the shock before the loudspeakers blare.

*"Battle stations, all hands! Enemy aircraft approaching thirty-five miles out! Prepare for attack!"*

"What?" I shout, same as half the men on board as we rush around to prepare. Those final wobbly Wildcats had been scrambled to try and meet this attack, which is a bad sign if there ever was one.

As the scene evolves, we can see what's happened, and what's happening. It's like a traveling air show as swarms of Japanese Zeroes and Vals tangle and dance in wild exchanges that are coming inevitably our way. The planes we've just sent are predictably slowing nothing as we realize these attackers have trailed some of our guys who were attempting to get back from the fight.

Aircraft from both sides go up in smoke and down in flames as the Pacific Ocean rapidly fills up with the finest engineering, and the finest men, America and the world have ever produced. But it is in no way an even match as the dogfighting moves ever closer and we see the numbers getting grimmer. The heavy guns pound away now that they are in range, the machine guns shade the sky all around us with shell bursts, and suddenly this doesn't look anything like victory.

With no obvious wave of our guys coming in to land, half the airedales are released to secondary battle stations, which has me rushing back down to the hangar deck for the fire crew. The gunfire and engine sounds are even more worrisome from down there where I cannot see it all, and though I don't quite reach the fire equipment and join the crew, the ship's public address system clarifies things for everyone.

*"Air department, take cover. Gunnery department, take cover. Prepare for attack!"*

Some of their bombers have broken through. We are going to be hit.

And I am alone, no matter how many people are around. No, I'm between.

Between one station and another, between one job and another. I feel like I'm in that limbo place that Mam called a crazy Catholic invention but still scared the pants off me.

My friends are in the sky, my family is back in the world. My ball club is disbanded. The only someone or something I feel truly and utterly a part of at this moment is above and below and all around and ultimately, inside me. *Yorktown.*

Everyone hits the deck and covers up wherever they are. I attempt to dive for the storage compartment where the fire gear is. I miss, as the bombs strike at the same time as my dive, and the storage compartment itself jerks out of my way as the floor rises to meet the side of my face.

I am holding my head, inching along the wall for no other reason than thinking wherever I go cannot feel as unsafe as the place I am now. Three bombs rumble above and below the hangar deck in rapid succession. The ship's sad stressed engines whine loudly as the captain tries desperately to repeat the magic tricks that helped us evade so many torpedoes in the Coral Sea. I raise my head as another bomb scores and see fire break out right up ahead of me on the hangar where the repair planes were and should still be.

I don't know what to do. I freeze where I am, watching the fire burn and waiting for that big loudspeaker voice to come up and tell me what I'm supposed to do right now. I listen in vain, but then the void is filled.

An unholy horror of an explosion erupts in the area of the great smokestack, and within seconds, my worst fears are confirmed when the ship's boilers go silent.

One of those rotten, amazing Japanese Val pilots has pinpointed a bomb right down the stack and blown the power right out of service.

There cannot be a more terrifying sensation than what we are experiencing now. All engines are out, lighting is out, and we float, a gigantic, powerless baby toy drifting in a lethal bath. Waiting. Waiting for all the worst things imaginable.

One of them comes immediately, as a bomb goes off a couple decks below. Another comes a half minute later when an explosion on the flight deck produces thunder above.

The planes depart. Having feasted on our big beautiful ship, the evil little bees buzz and hum for an excruciating duration as they withdraw. Listening to the sound shrink away feeds an anger in me I cannot compare with anything else I've known.

And as we float, dead in the water and unaided by any air cover, one thing is assured.

We've had their bombers. The torpedoes are yet to come.

Gradually, and then with more immediacy, crews get to work all over the ship. Any of our aircraft that have survived have been diverted to the other two carriers. Then, as we focus purely on the care of *Yorktown* herself, CAP squadrons from both *Hornet* and *Enterprise* fly continuous protection overhead to give us whatever chance we have of getting something going.

Fire crews are not going to go out of business any time soon, as we lurch from one blaze to the next on all decks continuously. Lights flicker back to life then out again as the electricians try to bring us out of the depths of darkness. Elsewhere, engineers bang and clang and tear and seal and do whatever it is they do, creating death-like but ultimately hopeful sounds of moaning down in the heart of the vessel, the boilers.

The public address system crackles, as first two, then three of the six boilers buck then hiss and crack back into life. We have power again, though truthfully very little of it. I rush to the open end of the hangar deck to get a feel for the situation and figure we are up to maybe fifteen knots.

That's not floating dead, but it's not much more than that.

It still feels close to a miracle that they're getting anything at all out of the old girl, and I'm grateful. There is some hope.

As soon as I let the thought take hold, it is tested in the worst way.

The CAP fighters above go into intercept mode, and I'm watching out the rear of the hangar deck as they soar into the teeth of the approaching group of enemy fighters and torpedo bombers. The loudspeaker commands all hands except gunnery to hit the deck, and this time I do so in a more orderly fashion. I sit cross-legged at the rail and watch the fierce dogfight play out. It is mayhem, and planes are shooting pieces out of each other like there is no tonight, never mind no tomorrow. Then the antiaircraft guns roar to life when four torpedo bombers break through and bear down on us. The first two drop their loads and are simultaneously blasted to pieces when they boldly bank right in the face of the big gunners. Both torpedoes barely skirt wide of us. Then the third one swoops, lines us up, and drops his sleek killer fish into the water and escapes. I watch the torpedo rocket toward us, displacing water ahead of it, and I flatten myself to the deck just as it's about to hit.

*Bu-boom!* It slams us with the sound and the impact of all the other bombs balled into one. It tears into our port side near amidships and practically lifts us out of the water before dropping us down gracelessly again. Men are screaming all over the ship as searing fire starts anew, and fuel oils somewhere are flooding, the smell strong and close.

I never see the second torpedo come in right next to the first one, and we twist violently, like a great hooked fish fighting with all it's got not to give in to the inevitable. Water mains burst all over the place, and our rudder locks us in a sickening and sad circle as we list fatally over about halfway onto our port side. I am scrambling like a crab, crawling on my hands, elbows, toes, to get away from the rail of the hangar deck, which is already touching the surface of the water.

It feels like I am climbing up the side of a building as I desperately claw my way away from the dirty ocean death that is lapping at the remaining souls of the magnificent USS *Yorktown*.

I reach a hole that's been torn in the deck by one of the explosions, and it's one of the million billion contradictions and ironies to have popped up in this war that

I see this bomb crater as my *salvation*. I crawl and stretch and just about get my fingers to the lip.

But the joke's on me as my reach comes up short, the many fluids bleeding out of the guts of the *Yorktown* running over the deck now and over me, and fouling my grip. I slide backward as abruptly, as quickly as if Poseidon or Davey Jones has me on a line and is yanking me down into the sea.

I slide, crawling and yelling and squirming all the way until I slam into the rail at the edge of the hangar deck where I spent so many days watching the water-world go by. I hit the rail flat backward, feel my spine jackknife violently in the wrong direction and somer-sault reverse, over, and into the salty ocean with a bang.

I rise to the surface several seconds later and find myself bobbing with several hundred other confused and desperate sailors. We all paddle madly, to escape from our great broken lady love who is burning, swirl-ing, disintegrating, and just might kill us all yet.

By the time I run out of paddling energy, I find myself bobbing on a relatively calm ocean. If the ship needed to give up now and go under, there would be nothing I could do to escape the draw because I am completely spent. I turn back and see the ship no longer circling in the near darkness, but just lying there. Around me I now realize are a lot more men than I had noticed before.

I am surrounded by a new small city as probably two-thirds of the crew of the *Yorktown* are floating in the waters around me. Some are screaming. Some are talking low, to themselves, to whomever they can get to listen. A whole lot of them are making no sounds at all.

This, right here, is the second-biggest population I've lived in. It's still more folks than all of Accokeek.

The water is warmer than I would have expected, and heavier. I should have been able to swim farther than this. I just stare at the ship, stare at its hulk of a silhouette as the light fades and the water seeps into my skin and makes me heavier, warmer, slower.

"Hey!" somebody screams right in my face and then slaps it, hard — forehand, backhand, forehand, backhand.

"Hey!" I shout back.

"Stay awake, stupid," he shouts, floating just inches away.

"I am awake," I say.

"You weren't. You were sleeping and you gotta not do that."

It's dark, but this close I can see him, his features all slurred, the lines of his face all thick with slime and grease. I raise my hand and realize I am covered in oil, from the bleeding ship. That is the warmth and heaviness that I feel. The sea is completely covered in it, as we all are.

"They'll be here soon," the guy insists. A dead sailor drifts over and into us and the guy shoves him away angrily as if the sailor was butting in on a private conversation. Almost as soon as he does, the dead body jerks horribly sideways, goes halfway under, then bobs up and drifts again.

"Sharks," the guy says, grabbing my chin hard for emphasis. "Just float, still as possible. This water is rotten with sharks. The explosions scared 'em off, now they're back. See the destroyers, just out there? They'll be close enough soon. Just hang on. And *don't fall asleep.*"

"I wasn't sleeping," I say.

"Well, you —"

"Holy — !" I say in terror as the corpse disappears with a splash and the shark's tail fin snaps at the water eight feet away.

More guys are screaming now, in the direction of the destroyers. The first of them are close enough that we can see the lights on board and the spotlights they are throwing down into the water. They have cargo nets hanging off their sides, and desperate men are using some superhuman reserves of strength to grab on and climb.

I do not know if I will have those reserves when my time comes. I do not know if my time will even come. The destroyers have to go so slowly just not to kill more men than they save.

Then, a separate pod of smaller vessels, whaling boats, is closing quickly from the opposite direction, dragging lines behind them. Those boats are already filled with soaking, oily survivors, the water lapping up over the sides of the overloaded whalers. They are hurrying toward the destroyers to unload before they sink, and the lines trailing are improvised tow lines for those desperate and lucky enough to snag them.

I make a move to start thrashing my way into the path of one of them.

"Don't!" the guy says, grabbing me hard enough to squeeze out half of my breath.

I am about to put up what little fight I can when the first whaler passes with a dozen guys dragging behind. Then a vicious slash cuts across the water, and across the whaler's line, and a massive shark takes a screaming and blood-bursting seaman by the waist and disappears with him beneath the whaler's wake.

I never heard such screaming from so many men.

Myself, I find that I cannot even manage that. I freeze, with fear, exhaustion, and stupidity. My muscles contract, my hands become useless claws, my shoulders hunch. I cannot look up, and I feel the oily, blood-sweet water rise up over my lips, drawing up into my nostrils.

I have never experienced pain in a dream before, but I believe that is what's happening when I suddenly find myself clinging to a cargo net as my hair is being pulled upward so hard pieces of my brain might come loose with it.

"Come on now, up we go, sailor!" I hear from above me as two of the destroyer's crew come almost down to the waterline to extract me from the water. I look around and behind me as I rise up the side of the ship, but I have no idea who it was pulling my hair to save my life.

One of the destroyer crew yanks me back violently in the direction of the deck.

"If you want to go back down there, just say the word and we'll drop you, sailor. But if you want to live, *come on!*"

CHAPTER EIGHT
# Hope

The survivors of the *Yorktown* were eventually plucked out of the sea by the various destroyers of Task Force 17. I was hauled up onto the *Balch*, which is now taxed to the limit by so many of us refugees. But the guys are all first rate and share their clothes and bits and pieces of candy and even their sleeping quarters as we all try and get shut-eye on a rotation system.

Without making a big deal of it I do a casual walking survey of who has made it with me onto the *Balch*. Many faces I recognize, many hands I shake. If the guy who saved my life is here I am ashamed to say I can't recognize him. I wouldn't be surprised if he is, and he's too much a real hero to say anything.

Other guys, guys I know better, are probably on other destroyers and we'll have a great reunion soon enough, with war stories aplenty.

The next day, the *Yorktown* has typically confounded all expectations by staying afloat. Sadly, she remains lamely on her side at the same list to port as when we left her.

When we awake to the same news again the following day, the destroyer's captain, Elliott Buckmaster, quickly organizes a salvage party, and I quickly get myself onto it.

We board the lady with the intention of stabilizing her as much as we can with an eye to possibly being able to save her. Another destroyer, the *Hamman*, pulls alongside and hooks up to provide power to the big carrier. Large teams are assigned the task of dumping as much bulk over the port side as possible to see how right she can get. Our enthusiasm grows when we find out the tug *Vireo* has been sent from Pearl Harbor to tow *Yorktown* back one more time to the miracle men of the shipyard there. There is actual, official hope now, and I can hardly contain my joy thinking about it. This is the story I have been holding out for. This is my against-all-odds redemption story that I will love to tell my people in the letters I finally feel I can write with both unlimited hopefulness, and honesty.

The battle here has been a monumental victory for us, and for the turning of the war against the now fatally depleted Japanese Imperial Navy. We know we hit them where we needed to.

But the story of the *Yorktown*, and her supernatural

survival over everything, that's our great victory. Mine and Theo's, Mam and Pop's.

Suzie's.

It is with a heavy heart that I join the search party to seek out and identify the dead on the lower decks. It is the very least a seaman can do for his shipmates. It is going to be harrowing, but at least I will know who is *not* here, who is still to be seen again elsewhere.

I am down on third deck, approaching the mess area. I will hope to see Bradford down here, cleaning up the mess of the mess and growling about the reasons for his being stuck so far down. I will hope for that until hope is impossible. And I will thank him for taking such good care of the gloves.

The ship does feel like it is moving up the right way. Maybe one degree. Maybe two. But the right way. This is slow and deliberate work, navigating treacherous, gutted corridors and fires that still burn slowly two days in. I am almost there, but proceed ever more slowly as I near the entrance to the mess, just being careful. Water is sloshing out of the mess and into the corridor.

And with the water comes the glove. I am foolishly excited to see the glove, waterlogged and sad as it is. I am as excited to see it as I was the first time I saw it, on that Christmas when Theo and I played the first game of catch that would lead to thousands and thousands more. It's Theo's glove, obvious with the new stitching even as soaked as it is. It makes me crazy stupid hopeful as I creep toward it.

*"Enemy submarine sighted, twelve hundred yards,"* the speakers squawk, making me jump out of and back into my skin.

"Somebody has a very sick sense of humor," I shout, in that furious tone you get when you are shocked out of your wits. The other salvage guys on deck three laugh nervously.

*Bu-hooom!*

Almighty goodness, that is a huge explosion right next door. We get rocked heavily as if a gigantic wave has just slammed us sideways. The power goes right out as the *Hamman* has apparently been torpedoed. It comes back on again briefly even as we hear the sounds of a destroyer sinking fast.

*"Torpedoes fired, twelve hundred yards! All hands down! All hands —"*

It's a line drive shot, apparently. A rocket, hit right toward second base.

# About the Author

Chris Lynch is the author of numerous acclaimed books for middle-grade and teen readers, including the Vietnam series and the National Book Award finalist *Inexcusable*. He teaches in the Lesley University creative writing MFA program and divides his time between Massachusetts and Scotland.